THE
HELL
BORN

THE
HELL
BORN

RAY HOGAN

THORNDIKE
CHIVERS

This Large Print edition is published by Thorndike Press®, Waterville, Maine USA and by BBC Audiobooks Ltd, Bath, England.

Published in 2005 in the U.S. by arrangement with Golden West Literary Agency.

Published in 2006 in the U.K. by arrangement with Golden West Literary Agency.

U.S. Hardcover 0-7862-7921-4 (Western)
U.K. Hardcover 1-4056-3651-3 (Chivers Large Print)
U.K. Softcover 1-4056-3652-1 (Camden Large Print)

The text of this Large Print edition is unabridged.
Other aspects of the book may vary from the original edition.

Set in 16 pt. Plantin.

Printed in the United States on permanent paper.

British Library Cataloguing-in-Publication Data available

Library of Congress Cataloging-in-Publication Data

Hogan, Ray, 1908–
   The hell born / by Ray Hogan.
      p. cm. — (Thorndike Press large print westerns)
   ISBN 0-7862-7921-4 (lg. print : hc : alk. paper)
   1. Prison wardens — Fiction.   2. Prisoners — Fiction.
3. Kidnapping — Fiction.   4. Escapes — Fiction.   5. Large
type books.   I. Title.   II. Thorndike Press large print
Western series.
PS3558.O3473H37 2005
   813'.54—dc22   2005014444

132717

THE
HELL
BORN

Standing well back in the mass of rocks that formed a sort of wall below the Territorial Prison, Billy Houston stirred restlessly. He glanced at his brother, Leo, at twenty a year his senior, and then at the lean, red-bearded older man crouched nearby.

"Jace, you figure we'll have to do some shooting?" he asked.

Jace Fargo swung his pale-blue eyes to the younger Houston, spat irritably. "You got something against putting a bullet in a couple of them damned screws?" he demanded, jerking a thumb in the direction of the guards stationed atop the penitentiary walls.

Leo Houston laughed. "Billy always was kind of lily-livered. He ain't never for shooting anything."

"The hell!" Billy replied angrily. "I'm just trying to think out how we're going to do this."

Fargo drew his pistol, rubbed its worn barrel and the indentations on the cylinder fondly. In his mid-forties, he had spent two-thirds of his life either behind bars or running from the law, and to him the life of any man was of little importance, much less if that particular man happened to have some connection with the law.

"We come here to get your pa," he said bluntly. "Whatever it takes — why, that's what we'll do."

"And that maybe'll call for killing three or four guards," Leo added, grinning.

Billy shrugged, listened briefly to the shrill bark of a prairie dog coming from the village on beyond the rocks. "I reckon that'd suit you fine, wouldn't it, Leo? Killing somebody's what you like."

"If they're needing it —"

Billy turned his glance to the gates in the prison's high wall. "Nope, you don't need a reason — only a excuse. I've been —"

"Hold off!" Fargo cut in wearily. "I've got me a bellyful of you two arguing back and forth. This here ain't the time for it. Soon as we get Rufe and light out, you can go right ahead, do all the jawing you're of a mind to. But right now it's best you keep your mind on business."

"Sure, Jace," Leo said agreeably, "it's only that I get mighty tired of him moaning and whining. Been that way all his life. Pa keeps saying he's like Ma and maybe he ought've been —"

"Shut up!" Billy snapped, picking up a rock. Light-haired, pale-eyed, and of slender build, he was the exact opposite of his brother, who favored their father. "You say that and I'll bash your damn head in!"

Leo considered Billy's set features for a long breath, shrugged, and shifted his attention back to Fargo. "You been watching goings-on around here for quite a spell; you for sure Pa'll be coming by here?"

"Today for sure," Jace said, sliding his weapon back into its holster. "The warden — name's Ben Skerrit — is showing off for the governor and some of them highfalutin, muckity-muck politician friends of his'n. Him and the governor wants them all to see how this here new idea of how to run a pen works. Rufe and about a dozen others'll be marching right by here on the way to that orchard there at the bottom of the hill."

"How many guards'll be along with them?" Leo asked.

"Three, maybe four. There'll be another work party going down the trail to the garden. Can figure on there being that many screws with it."

Leo stared off at a low bank of gray clouds gathering along the eastern horizon.

After a bit he shook his head. "Just seems awful easy — too damn easy, in fact. Pa and them could jump the guards, take off —"

"That's what this here's all about! The warden's picked the cons who've been real good boys and ain't caused no trouble to work outside — and they all been put on their honor."

Leo Houston laughed. "And Pa's one of them?"

Fargo nodded. "Yes, sir, he sure is. Old Rufe wasn't behind the door when the brains was passed out. Minute they locked them gates behind him, he started reforming. He never done nothing to rile the screws and it was 'yes, sir' and 'no, sir' to everybody. And he was mighty helpful, too."

"How long was you and him partnering?"

"Well, I was winding up my five-year stretch. Had about a year to go, maybe a bit longer, when he come in. Reckon that's it, about a year and a half."

"Wasn't the same warden running the place when you were there, though, was it?"

"Nope, was a hard-nosed son of a bitch named Monahan in charge then. About the meanest sucker I ever come up against. He run the place with a sawed-off scatter-gun in one hand and a blacksnake whip in the other. Somebody finally got him, however. Stuck a knife in his belly and spilled his guts all over the floor of his office one day."

"One of the convicts?"

"Ain't nobody sure, but word got around that it was a screw that done it. Seems Monahan had been fooling around with his woman."

Leo laughed. "Ain't much to kill a man over, is it, Billy?" he said, slanting a look at his brother. "You be willing to kill a man for fiddling around with your wife, if ever you get one?"

"Maybe," Billy said indifferently. "Leastwise, that'd be a good reason. . . . What time'll they be coming, Jace?" he continued, looking up at the prison perched on the crest of the hill, bleak and barren in the sunlight.

Fargo glanced to the east, gauged the hour. It was well into midmorning. "Pretty soon, I expect. Them work parties always gets a early start. Could be they'll be a mite late today — getting paraded around like they are."

Leo grinned, rubbed at his jaw. "This sure is going to spoil the warden's whoop-de-do, Pa busting out."

"Yeh, and that's something we've got to make certain of. Can't afford no slipups. You both got it straight in your heads what you're to do?"

Leo nodded. "Hashed it over with myself a full dozen times," he replied, and glanced at Billy. "How about you?"

The younger Houston stirred. "Reckon I know what I'm to do."

Fargo spat again, changed his position. The prisoners would be passing within only a few yards of where he and Houston's two sons had hidden themselves shortly before dawn that morning, and unless something unforeseen occurred, they would have no problems.

"Your pa'll be the last in the line," Fargo said, deciding it was only prudent to review the escape plan for a final time. "He's making sure that he will be. There'll be a screw behind him — maybe two. Soon as Rufe and them pass, we jump out quick and cold-cock the screws.

"We knock them out with the butts of our guns. No shooting because, if we do this right, we won't even draw no attention. It'll be me and you, Leo, that jumps out and slams them over the head. Rufe'll be looking sharp for us to make the move, and when he sees us, he'll head in our direction.

12

You'll run to meet him, Billy, and have a gun in your hand ready for him.

"Soon as he's got it and we've took care of them guards — or the guard — we all duck back into these here rocks. If we don't make no big fuss them screws up at the front of the line won't even know what happened, but if they do, we'll be in here behind the rocks and they'll be out there in the open. Can cut them down quick and light out for the horses."

"Some of them other convicts are going to see what's going on and want to throw in with Pa," Leo said. "We letting them?"

"They ain't coming with us," Fargo said, shaking his head. "First off, we ain't got but four horses — and we won't have no time to waste riding double. Getting away from here real fast is going to be mighty important."

Billy was once more studying the high stone wall of the prison. Smoke was rising from somewhere within the forbidding enclosure, twisting up in a slender, gray column. His pa had been in there for well over two years now, serving a sentence of life for murder. But shortly that would end; Rufe would be out — and free again.

Billy sighed inwardly. He could almost wish it wasn't true. He had never felt anything but fear and hatred for his pa, and without him he and Leo had done fairly well robbing a bank in some small town now and then or holding up a stage-coach or a general store somewhere. Now Leo, who was a pretty good fellow when he wasn't around their pa, would turn back into the old Leo, a hateful, walking, talking shadow of Rufe — had already done so, in fact — and they would be forced to throw in with Pa and Jace Fargo and do things their way.

And unless Rufe had changed, which wasn't at all likely, that meant a lot of hell-for-leather riding, killing, looting, robbing, and rape, if some woman or girl was unfortunate enough to be handy.

He wished now that he and Leo had pulled up stakes and left the country a year ago when they'd talked about it. But they'd let it pass and then Jace Fargo had come along with the scheme for an escape that he and Rufe had worked out and it was too late. If only . . .

"Gate's opening." Fargo's laconic words broke the warm hush. "They'll be coming, so get yourself ready."

2

Ben Skerrit heaved a sigh of relief and sat down. He was no hand at making speeches, but Horn, the governor, had insisted that he detail, to the territorial officials and newspaper representatives present, his theory of prison operation. Now it was over, and brushing at the sweat collected on his forehead, he readied himself for the questions he felt certain would come next. And come they did, immediately.

"Warden, do you really think you can put men like the ones you have in here on their honor and trust them to observe it?"

Skerrit smiled thinly. The man speaking was Henry Morrison, the governor's aide. The question he had set forth no doubt had been planted in his mind by Burt Horn in order to more fully clarify the changes that had been instituted at the prison.

"Not all, of course," he replied. "There are some inside the walls of this pen — as well as outside — that couldn't be trusted across this room."

There was a ripple of laughter, and someone in the two dozen or so persons attending the meeting clapped appreciatively. Horn, well pleased, nodded to Skerrit.

"Warden, we'll all take it as a favor if you'll stand and tell just what prompted you to make the changes you've put in effect here."

Skerrit sighed again, came slowly to his feet. A tall man, muscular, with dark hair and level gray eyes, he looked out over the room. Cigar smoke hung thick in the warm, trapped air, and now and then someone coughed.

"Yuma — that's what set me to thinking," he said, nodding slightly to one of the trusties who, noting the heavy cloud in the room, had opened one of the shuttered windows. "I was a lawman before I took this job — a sheriff. Made several trips to the pen at Yuma and got a first-hand look at how the prisoners there lived — or I best say, existed."

"Most men in prison are there for good reason," a voice in the back commented. "Murder, robbery — crimes like those. They're not supposed to be treated like they were at a Sunday sociable."

"Can't argue that," Skerrit replied. "They're here for punishment — paying

16

with the years of their lives for something they've done — and the majority of them are not entitled to be included in our rehabilitation program."

"*Rehabilitation,* that's a new word —"

"Been around for a long time," Skerrit said dryly. "Just happens nobody ever used it much. . . . Now, gentlemen, don't misunderstand me. I'm not soft on the convicts in this pen, but I do believe that it's smart to give a hand to the ones who are repentant and are anxious to start over, make a new life for themselves."

"You think that's possible?" Henry Morrison wondered aloud. "You actually believe you can take a murderer and turn him into a decent, law-abiding citizen simply by providing work for him in a garden or whatever else it is you do for them?"

"I can answer that," Governor Horn snapped, casting an angry glance at his assistant as he came to his feet. Horn was counting heavily on the favorable publicity that Skerrit's prison-reform plan would receive — hopefully — to boost his political future.

"We have seen several living proofs of its value already," Horn said. "Three men who were serving terms in here for crimes they committed have been released — at the expiration of their terms, of course — have gone back into the world with trades they learned here under the supervision of Warden Skerrit.

"Under the usual system they would have been turned loose no better off for the time they spent inside these walls. But now they have a trade, a skill, and have gone out and become useful citizens since it will no longer be necessary for them to turn to crime for a living."

"Makes sense," a voice said.

"Yeh, does, unless the jasper's just a natural outlaw and don't want to be nothing else."

"What about that, Warden? You admit there are some that your scheme — rehabilitation or whatever you call it — won't work with?"

Skerrit's mouth was a hard, straight line as he gave that thought. Finally he shrugged. "I'm not going to say that we can help every man in here — or that there's anything we can do about them once they've served their time or have been pardoned. That would be foolish.

"But we do everything possible to help any man who wants to be helped and teach him a trade with the aid of the facilities we have."

"I intend to ask the legislature for more money to give Warden Skerrit so that he can increase the number of trades offered here," Horn said, smiling.

Skerrit nodded to Burt Horn. "My thanks, Governor. It will be a big help. There are at least five more trades that we could teach if we had the means, and being able to offer them I know we can interest even more prisoners in the program."

"That mean you've got a lot of prisoners in here who refuse to take a hand in it?"

"Only natural that we do. And we don't force any man to take part. It's up to them. They're required to do only the tasks assigned to them by the guards."

"Then ain't it likely a lot of them who are in your program are doing it so's they can dodge the jobs they'd ordinarily have to do like policing the place, digging latrines, carrying slop, and such?"

"It would be more than likely, but that's not how it is. They still have their share of prison duties to perform. After all, as one of you said, these men are in here being punished for a crime they've committed."

There was a few moments of silence and then a tall, graying man got to his feet. Tyler, one of the newspaper reporters, Skerrit recalled. Burt Horn particularly wanted to impress him and gain his support.

"I'm not so sure about this plan of yours, Warden," Tyler said doubtfully. "I've never heard of anything like it being tried before — anywhere. Could be you're putting your faith in the wrong kind of men. There's an old saying — you can't make a pet of a rattlesnake — and I'm wondering if maybe it applies here."

"I can only point to the record," Skerrit said. "So far none of the men we've trained have gotten into trouble, not one! And —"

"And that's what this is all about," Horn cut in. "We're simply trying to make it possible for men who leave here to have a way of making their living and not be compelled to fall back on their old habits, which would eventually put them inside prison walls again, here or somewhere else.

"And the warden hasn't mentioned that his plan cuts down the territory's cost of running the prison. They now raise their vegetables and fruit — which saves the government a considerable amount — and still have some to sell."

"What happens to the money they get for it?" Tyler asked quickly, suspiciously.

"Every cent is accounted for," the governor replied coldly. "It goes into a fund that is used to buy supplies needed to teach the trades offered. Naturally the amount is small and the fund grows slowly, as most of the produce ends up on the table right here. But you can take my solemn word for it, Mr. Tyler, not one copper goes into anyone's pocket."

"We hope eventually to buy cattle, start raising our own beef," Skerrit said, hoping to bridge the tension that Tyler's question had given rise to. "We now have a few hogs along with some chickens and turkeys, but we need to get into the cattle business, not only for the meat but for the hides as well. There is a good market for leather."

"Where'll you get grazing land?" a man, obviously a rancher from his dress, asked. "What I've seen around here sure ain't worth much."

"I admit that, but we can get three hundred and twenty acres close by for practically nothing. It won't support more than one cow to maybe twenty acres now, but we can change that by drilling a well and putting up a windmill. Water will make all the difference —"

"Always does," the cattleman said. "Grass'll grow overnight if there's water. Should be able to run a half a dozen cows to the acre if you handle it right."

"All of which will take a lot of money,"

Horn said, smiling broadly, "but it can be done if the legislature will cooperate. . . . Now, gentlemen, if there are no more questions, I'd like to get on with it. I asked the warden to hold back the parties that work the fields and orchards so that you can get a look at them as they march by. If ever you saw hope and happiness on the faces and in the eyes of men who, under other circumstances, would think of themselves as having no future, you'll see it now. . . . All right, Warden, we're ready."

Skerrit nodded, moved away from the table behind which he had been sitting with the governor, and started for the door. Much depended on the next hour, he knew, for many of the men present who were influential in the legislature, along with several of the newspapermen, were far from convinced that his plan was workable.

But he was confident that, if they would take note of the prisoners involved as they passed by and then later watch them at their labors in the fields and orchards, they would have to admit that his efforts toward rehabilitation were worthwhile.

"Just follow me," he said. "You can see it all for yourself."

3

"You see Pa yet?" Leo Houston asked in a low, tense voice.

Neither Fargo nor Billy made a reply. They had all moved forward in the massive pile of rocks, were now crouched nearer to the trail, and, weapons drawn and ready, were watching the two columns of prisoners file slowly through the gates in the wall into the open.

"What're all them dudes doing up there?" Leo again voiced a question.

"Like I've done said," Jace Fargo answered impatiently, "this here's a special day at the pen — that's why Rufe and me picked it for the break. Tipped me off soon's he heard when it was to be so's we could be here waiting."

"What's making it special? Don't recollect you saying."

"The governor's showing all his friends what a fine job the warden's doing at making them convicts over into good, law-abiding citizens. Guess he's got them standing there at the gate so's they'll get a close look."

"What if they decided to follow Pa and them?"

"Ain't much chance. It's getting hot and it'd be a long walk down to the fields. They'd all get their boots dusty and —"

"There's Pa," Billy said.

Fargo nodded. "Just like we schemed it up — he's the last in the line. And there's only one screw behind him. Makes it real easy for us."

There were twenty prisoners, single file, in the column winding slowly down the slope from the crest of the hill. One guard was at its head, a second had taken a place midway along its length, and a third brought up the rear. That there were so few armed men with the convicts was clearly a demonstration of trust on the part of the warden and meant to impress the outsiders looking on.

"Pa sure don't look no different," Leo said. "Just as big and ornery as ever."

"Told you Rufe'd make out, no matter what. I'll lay odds that he's the warden's pet," Fargo said, laughing as he swiped at the sweat shining on his ruddy face. "Now, we're going to have to do some changing. There's only one screw following your pa. Means only one of us will have to move in behind him — and that'll be me. Still figure on you getting a gun to Rufe real quick, howsomever, Billy."

"So what'll I be doing?" Leo demanded, frowning.

"You keep an eye on them other screws — especially the one there in the middle. Better watch out for them jaspers near your pa, too. Can bet a couple of them'll try to go with him."

"That'll be a mighty fast way to die," Leo said, nodding. "Ain't none of them going with us."

Fargo gave Leo a direct look, shook his head. "I said there'd be no shooting, and I meant it — not that I give a damn about you putting a bullet in one of them cons or guards — it's that we don't want to draw no attention. You don't pull that trigger unless you have to."

"Don't see as that'll matter much once Pa's with us and's got a gun in his hand. We can take on all comers then."

Billy Houston's eyes were on the approaching column of men, now only fifty yards or so distant. Beyond them he could see the governor's party, all well-dressed men, still clustered about the entrance to the prison. The two lines of convicts, the one heading down the other side of the hill for the gardens and the one drawing near as it made its way for the orchards, were now well clear of the gates. Shortly the former would be out of sight as it dropped behind the crown of the slope.

High above the stone buildings on the top of the hill several buzzards were circling lazily as they awaited the garbage detail's activity, and the column of smoke had thickened, was now a sooty black. The barely audible whistle of a meadowlark rode the motionless air, coming to them from the direction of the fields.

"You all set?" Fargo asked in a tight voice.

The guard at the head of the column was now only steps away, a thin, red-faced man with a full beard and mustache. Muscles tensed, Billy remained silent. The guard drew abreast, passed on by, trailed by the trudging convicts: a black; a squat, hairy-looking Mexican; a thick-armed man who might have been a blacksmith; a boy no older than himself; others, varying in age, build, and facial expression. And then his pa was moving by.

Big, with bristling dark beard and mustache, Rufe's small, black eyes were hard and glittering like agates and his jaw was set while his large hands clenched and released spasmodically. His skin was almost as dark as his hair from constant exposure to the sun, and his teeth contrasted whitely between heavy, thick lips. His glance was to the side — toward the rocks — but it was furtive, so as to not excite the suspicion of either the guards or his fellow prisoners.

Rufe passed on. The man trailing him — a lean, quiet-faced individual in a worn, blue uniform, rifle slung in the crook of his left arm, hat tipped forward to shield his eyes from the sun — drew abreast, moved by.

"Now," Jace Fargo murmured.

As one the three men rose from the rocks and slipped in quickly and quietly behind the column. Billy saw Fargo close with the unsuspecting guard, smash his pistol down on the man's head with sickening force. Leo, crouched low, surged forward.

"Pa," he called softly.

At once Houston pivoted. Billy met him straight on, thrust a pistol into his hands. The convict immediately in front of Rufe, hearing the slight scuffling, wheeled. A wide grin split his mouth.

"You're breaking out! I'm going with you!"

"The hell you are!" Rufe snarled and struck the man across the head with his weapon.

The convict yelled in pain as he began to

fall. Instantly the line halted and the prisoners began to mill about uncertainly. A shout went up.

"Stand where you are!" one of the guards commanded. "Move and you're dead!"

"You're the dead one, Gabe!" Rufe Houston yelled, and drove a bullet into the man.

At once Houston wheeled, began to run for the rocks. The remaining guard brought up his rifle, leveled it.

"Watch out, Pa!" Leo shouted, and snapped a shot at the uniformed man.

The bullet caught the guard in the leg, spun him half about, dropped him to his knees. Elsewhere, the remaining prisoners were scattering, some racing for the rocks, others for the brush farther down the slope.

Back up at the prison men were calling out and Billy could see more guards coming through the gates, having been summoned from their duties elsewhere within the walls. Shortly a search party would get under way for Rufe and for the others in the column who had rushed into hiding during the confusion.

"Come on!" Billy heard Fargo yell. "We got to get out of here!"

Bending low, Billy started for the rocks. A few steps ahead of him he could see Rufe. Fargo and Leo were a bit behind and to his right. Dust stirred up along the trail by hurrying feet now hung in a yellow cloud above the men sprawled on the ground — a convict and three guards — and all but two of the remaining prisoners who had been in the column had disappeared.

"Where's the horses?" Rufe shouted as they came together in the rocks.

"On down the wash a ways," Leo answered, brushing at the sweat misting his eyes. "Sure good to see —"

"A ways!" Rufe echoed. "Damn it, how far's that?"

"Fifty, sixty feet maybe," Leo said. "Just keep following me."

Abruptly his stride broke. A man, one of the escaping convicts, had appeared suddenly at the edge of the arroyo down which they were running.

"Rufe!" he gasped, sucking hard for wind. "I'm sure glad it's you! I'm going with —"

"We ain't got no extra horse," Rufe replied.

"Hell, I can ride double with the kid there," the man said. "I don't weigh much — no more'n him. It won't slow you down none."

Rufe looked down at the man, now keeping pace at his shoulder. "Said no, Charlie —"

"You can't, Rufe! You owe me a couple of favors. Was that time —"

"Sure do thank you, sucker," Rufe said, and twisting about, shot the man dead. Avoiding the falling body, he turned again to Leo. "Where's them damned horses? You told me —"

"Right around that there bend ahead, Pa. That's where Billy tied them up. It's as close as we dared put them."

"Good thing. They got horses back there for them screws to ride. They'll be down here mighty soon."

Leo, out in front, rounded the shoulder in the arroyo and pulled up short. As the others drew up beside him, he turned to them, face blank.

"The horses — they ain't here!"

Skerrit led the way through the entrance to his combined office and living quarters and out onto the porch that fronted it. He threw a quick look around the prison yard. The work parties were still standing about, waiting to be marched to their respective jobs in the fields and orchards.

They had been ready for hours, he knew, and he felt a stir of anger at himself for having held the men up and keeping them from their labors, but it had been the governor's idea and he'd gone along with it — not so much for the sake of Burt Horn's political future but, frankly, in the hope that the end result would mean a larger appropriation for the penitentiary.

One thing he did wish was that the governor would soon end what he chose to term a demonstration in good management. It was disrupting prison routine, and that was not good.

Moving down the steps, Ben Skerrit struck out across the hard-packed yard for the massive gates in the stone walls. He felt the eyes of nearby prisoners on him and the men trailing him as he strode quickly toward the opening; and the thought came to him that it would be an ideal time, with so many visitors present and most daily procedures suspended as they were, for some of the old hard cases to try and escape.

Not all prisoners had resigned themselves to life inside the walls, and Skerrit was smart enough to know that many never would and that, given an opportunity, they would make an effort to break out. He had neutralized that possibility to some extent, he felt, by creating jobs open to all and allowing those who proved themselves trustworthy to work on the outside.

By granting such to the men anxious to pass the time more quickly as well as learn a trade while doing so, Skerrit believed their appreciation would serve as a check on the unruly and incorrigible ones who fomented trouble. He had made it clear to all that all welfare programs would be canceled immediately should any man take advantage of his trust and attempt an escape. So far no convict had made an effort — a fact of which Ben Skerrit was justifiably proud.

He reached the gates, motioned to the sentries on duty to swing them open, and turned to face the men accompanying him. The governor, having been at the rear of the group, immediately forged to the fore and took up a stand beside Skerrit.

"I want to mention again that you will see in the faces and eyes of the convicts who will be passing by you on their way to work, a look of hope as well as one of gratification to Warden Skerrit for what he is doing for them."

Tyler, the newspaperman, shrugged, lit a cigar. "Can understand that, Governor. I'd be grateful, too — getting out from behind these walls."

The rancher, his stogie already lit, bobbed. "Who wouldn't? I can't hardly stand the inside of my house more'n a couple of hours."

Everyone laughed except Skerrit, who had turned his attention to the guards overseeing the work parties. He nodded and at once the uniformed men gave a command. The waiting convicts stirred, roused, began to form twin lines. A second order was given, and the columns, with guards in front, on the side, and at the rear, moved forward. As they approached the gates, Tyler shifted his attention to Ben Skerrit.

"I see they're not carrying tools. They do

all this work you talked about with their bare hands?"

"Hardly," the warden replied in an even voice. The newspaperman irritated him, and he was having difficulty in not showing it. Ordinarily he wouldn't give a damn but Tyler's paper was widely read and wielded considerable influence.

"We send the tools on ahead in one of the wagons."

"Just don't want to tire the boys out, that it?" Tyler persisted in the same ironic tone.

"No," Skerrit said. "I just don't think it's a good idea to put temptation in their way. A hoe, a spade, tools like that can become dangerous weapons if something happened to set a man off —"

"Then you admit your whole program is risky?"

"I've never said it wasn't," Skerrit answered coolly. "There's no guarantee that something unexpected won't happen that will upset the plan —"

"Upset!" Tyler repeated. "That's a hell of a poor word to use for something that would probably end in killings!"

"It hasn't occurred yet," Burt Horn declared, cutting himself in on the conversation. "And I don't think it will as long as these men are being treated as human beings and allowed to spend their time learning and doing something constructive. . . . Look at them! You see the sign of trouble on the faces of any of them?"

Morrison, silent for some time, said, "Nope, I sure don't."

Tyler eyed the governor's aide in amusement. "How can you tell, Henry? What's trouble in the making look like?"

"I'll tell you," the governor said at once, stepping in for Morrison. "There'll be anger for one thing. Tightens the muscles of the face and makes the eyes hard as rocks. And sullenness — that's a sure sign. You agree, Warden?"

Skerrit's wide shoulders stirred. It was the same as being asked what a murderer looked like — as if one always bore some definite mark that distinguished him as such. But it was best — and smart — to go along with Horn.

"If a man's not satisfied, it shows up in a lot of ways, all right."

The governor nodded. "True. Now, do any of you see any sullenness or dissatisfaction in those men marching by?"

There was a murmur of denial. The rancher exhaled a cloud of smoke, said, "No, I can't say that any of them looked real happy, but on the other hand I reckon they weren't what you'd call sullen. You got a point, Burt?"

"Exactly," the governor replied. "It's that prisoners who aren't down at the mouth, sullen, and such are prisoners that won't give you trouble."

The rancher nodded his agreement. Tyler shrugged, murmured, "I suppose you're right."

"You can bet money on it," Horn said flatly.

The last men in the two columns, one heading for a day of work in the gardens, the others for the orchards, were passing through the gates, each with its armed guard bringing up the rear. Skerrit looked back into the prison yard. The remaining convicts had resumed their regular chores — raking, cleaning their quarters, washing clothes, building furniture, and various other tasks.

Over beyond the barracks three of the men had gotten the small steam engine running that he had persuaded the government to buy, and were using it to split wood for the kitchen and laundry. Smoke was coming from the chimney of the former, where the cook and his helpers were preparing the noon meal.

The food was to be special today, thanks

to the presence of the governor and his guests, and Skerrit reckoned he'd best drop by the kitchen and see that matters were progressing as they should. So far the visit of Horn and his friends had gone well; he'd hate to have it spoiled at the last minute by a mix-up of some kind.

"Hey!" One of the men in the crowd gathered at the gates yelled suddenly. "Something's happening down there!"

Skerrit whirled. Tyler and several of the visitors were pushing by him out onto the sloping crown of the hill. As he looked, Ben saw the guard who had been the last in the column going to the orchards fall to the ground. Three men had appeared — evidently coming from the rocks to the west of the trail — and were attacking the guards.

Coming back around, Skerrit shouted to the assistant warden standing on the porch of his quarters. "Sound the alarm bell — we've got a break under way! And send some guards over here!"

The man nodded. Grasping the rope that activated the bell in the tower above him, he began to jerk it, all the while yelling orders. Skerrit, anger surging through him, turned back to the gates, put his attention on the activity down the hill.

One of the convicts, a big man — Houston, Ben thought his name was but he couldn't be absolutely certain because of the distance — had pulled away from the other prisoners. He now had a pistol in his hand. That it was not a break made on the spur of the moment was clear; it had been carefully planned, and the three men who had laid in wait in the rocks were a part of it.

Another prisoner had left the column, beginning to break up, was hurrying toward Houston. He appeared to be joining the big man and his friends, but Houston abruptly clubbed him over the head and dropped him to the ground. Houston pivoted then, fired point-blank at another guard, then spun and began to run for the rocks.

The uniformed men summoned from elsewhere inside the walls were now arriving, pausing in the opening, and awaiting his instructions. Skerrit pointed to the dusty confusion. The rest of the prisoners were scattering as the third guard had been shot and had gone to his knees.

"Get down there!" the warden shouted. "They're running into the rocks and the brush. Couple of you better use horses. There's twenty men in the work party — and I want every damn one of them back in here before dark!"

Ben Skerrit's voice was harsh, his face set to grim lines. The thought, There's always one son of a bitch around to spoil a good thing, was rushing through his mind. Houston! He was the one the three outsiders had come to help. Damn him to hell anyway!

"What about the bunch at the garden?"

The voice brought Ben around. It was the assistant warden. "Get them back here — this could spread, set off a general break," he replied, curbing the anger in his voice. He shifted his glance to Burt Horn. "Governor, I'm going to have to take a hand in this. I want you and your guests to go over to the mess hall and stay inside until things quiet down a bit."

Tyler, cigar clamped in a corner of his mouth, was fumbling with his collar, running a finger around inside it, as if finding it too tight. "You sure we'll be safe there?" he asked.

"As safe there as anywhere."

The rancher spat, shook his head. "That's the way to put it, all right. No place'll be guarantee safe for a spell. Reckon this proves one thing — you just can't bank on men. Some are just plain hell-born and don't ever change."

"And mollycoddling them doesn't help," Tyler added pointedly. "All this do-gooder treatment just makes it easy for them to someday escape."

Burt Horn took the newspaperman by the arm and, turning him about, started back into the compound. Pointing to the mess hall, he said, "Let's do what the warden suggested. Can maybe promote ourselves a cup of coffee."

"I sure as hell could use something a mite stronger," the rancher said as the entire party began to move through the gates, now being closed.

Horn, clearly showing strain but striving to make the best of a bad situation, managed a smile. "I'll see what I can do, Parley," he said, and as his guests continued on their way, paused and, solemn-faced, looked over his shoulder at Skerrit. "Keep me posted."

The chill and accusation in the governor's voice was not lost on Ben — the blame for what had happened was all his, rested squarely on his shoulders. It was as plain as if written in red.

Anger and frustration whipped through him, brought a sharp reply to his lips. But he let it die and, shrugging, put his attention again on the dust-shrouded slope below.

"They sure ain't here!" Jace Fargo said, breathing hard. "Was right there by that cedar. Seen Billy tie them up myself."

Rufe Houston, broad, dark face taut, eyes hard, wheeled to his younger son. "You just don't never change, do you?" he shouted.

"I tied them good, Pa," Billy replied, retreating a step before his father's fury.

"Like hell you did! They'd be standing there right now if you'd done it right," Rufe said. "You never could do nothing right — never could depend on you!"

"Told you I tied them good," the younger Houston said doggedly. "Somebody —"

"That's you all over — go blaming somebody else," Rufe cut in, and suddenly raising his arm, slapped Billy hard across the side of the head. "When're you going to grow up to be a man?"

Billy staggered, caught himself, and glared at his parent. "I tied them good —"

"Rufe," Fargo broke in hurriedly, "we best be getting out of here. Them screws'll be showing up."

"How we doing that?" Leo asked. "We ain't got nothing to ride."

"Walk — that's how," Rufe stated. "Maybe run if we have to — thanks to your brother."

"If them horses strayed, could be we'll be coming across them," Fargo said, hopefully as they started down the wash.

"Maybe," Rufe said, throwing a cold-eyed glance at Billy. "Can't see why you let him take care of the horses, Leo. You know same as me he can't be trusted to do nothing right."

Leo shook his head. "He tied them up, Pa," he said more in defense of himself than his brother. "I'm wondering if somebody didn't come along and steal them. Could have been some of them other convicts."

"Ain't likely," Fargo said. "They couldn't've got ahead of us that far. I'm betting it was drifters."

They had quickened their pace to a run and sweat was now dampening their clothing and shining on their skins. Rufe brushed at his forehead, looked back in the direction of the prison. It was set high above its surrounding area and the structure with its thick stone walls was clearly visible, but the outlaw could not see the slope

42

flowing down from it where the actual break had taken place.

"Let's get out of this here arroyo," Fargo said. "Them screws'll be looking in here for us first off."

Immediately Rufe veered and, crossing to the west side of the wash, climbed its low bank to the brushy flat above. Again wiping away the sweat on his face, he halted.

"I've run plumb out of wind. Got to slow down a mite."

Jace Fargo was staring back over the course they had come. "Can see somebody moving off there a piece. Ain't sure if it's one of the cons or somebody else."

Rufe, with Billy and Leo, turned their attention to where Fargo pointed. "Jasper on a horse," Leo said promptly.

"That'd be one of the screws," Rufe said. "Can see him myself now. He's nabbed one of the cons and's heading back to the hill with him."

"Good," Fargo said, mopping at his face and neck with a bandanna. "Means they ain't got a search going good yet — still sort of close in. Gives us more time."

"We'll be needing it," Rufe said dourly, glancing at Billy. "That Sunday-school-marm warden'll be looking hard to find me. Expect he seen it was me that busted

43

up his little party and plugged that screw. He'll be just a-honing to see me swing for it. . . . Got to get away from here fast — find some horses. There a ranch or maybe a town somewheres close?"

"Batesville," Billy said sullenly, speaking for the first time since Rufe had struck him. "Eight or nine mile west of here."

Rufe looked for confirmation from Leo. "He right?"

"Reckon so. Ain't no town, just a general store and a couple of houses."

"We're going to be needing everything," Fargo said, again staring off toward the prison. "Had our grub, blankets, everything on them horses."

Rufe swore, glared at Billy, and nodded. "Ain't nothing to do then but light out for this here Batesville, get ourselves fixed up there."

"We ain't got much cash money —"

"Don't figure on spending any," Rufe said, patting the pistol thrust under his waistband. "Aim to do my paying with this. . . . We still got that deal waiting for us across the border?"

"Sure have," Jace replied. "Jaramillo's just holding up till we get there."

"What deal?" Leo asked. "I sure ain't heard nothing about no deal in Mexico."

44

"Me neither," Billy said. The anger and resentment that had claimed him earlier was finally wearing off.

"Mostly because I ain't told you about it yet," Fargo said. "Figured first things come first — and that was getting your pa out of the pen. Me and him've had it a-cooking for quite a spell."

"What is it?" Leo pressed. "I ain't all that crazy going down into Mexico. The stinking Federales once —"

"Reckon you'll do what I tell you," Rufe cut in bluntly. "But I expect you'll be liking the idea. It's for gold, a hell of a lot of gold."

"Yeh?" Leo said, interest quickening.

"Right — a lot of gold, just like your pa said," Fargo continued. "Friend of mine down there — Mex named Jaramillo — him and his boys've got a gold mine and a smelter in the Sierra Madre all staked out. Says it's just ripe for the taking."

Leo had pulled off his hat, was running stubby fingers through his shock of dark hair. "Why don't this Jaramillo and his bunch go right ahead on their own? Why they being so ding-dang nice to us?"

"Well, old Sosteen — that's Jaramillo's front name — needs help to pull it off and he don't trust none of his *compadres*. Besides, he owes me a favor — that's how come we're in on it. But he ain't going to hold off much longer. If we don't show up by the first of the month, I expect he'll figure out something else."

"Gives us a couple of weeks," Rufe said, "and it's going to be worth plenty to all of us. More'n we can ever use, likely. You boys can come back here, if you don't cotton to Mexico, do whatever you please with your share. Me, I'll have to stay on there, on the other side of the border, where the law can't nail me."

"You won't be minding that, Rufe," Fargo said with a laugh.

"Nope, I reckon I won't — not with all them pretty little Mex *señoritas* and good liquor to pass the time with. . . . I've rested enough. Let's get moving."

"Expect we better," Fargo said, "but first we ought to see to them tracks we left in the wash. Ain't no sense in making it easy for them screws that'll be trailing us."

"For certain," Rufe said, looking out over the flat to the west, shimmering in the sunlight. "I want you boys to cut yourselves off a couple of branches from one of them rabbit bushes, then go back in the wash and start sweeping out our footprints."

"Find a place where it's kind of rocky," Fargo added. "Make the trail end there.

Just sort of let the tracks lead up to —"

"Guess I've wiped out tracks before," Leo said stiffly. "I don't need no lessons on how to do it."

Rufe Houston's mouth parted into a hard grin. "Maybe not, but you're sure needing some learning about not sassing your elders."

Leo, in the act of cutting a branch from a nearby shrub, paused, looked squarely at his parent. "I ain't no kid, Pa, not anymore. I'm most twenty-one and I —"

"Long as you're around me you'll do what I tell you," Rufe snapped, "else you'll get same as what Billy got! Now, hustle your tails, both of you, and take care of that there trail like Jace told you to. And you be damn sure there ain't no sign showing where we climbed out of the wash."

Leo, a branch of the bush in his hand, again hesitated, put his attention on Rufe. He seemed about to make further comment, but he apparently thought better of it and, jerking his head at Billy, now also equipped with a bit of brush, turned away.

"Let's get to doing it," he said.

"And don't you go taking too long!" Rufe called after them. "The border's a far piece from here and I want to get started."

6

"You calling that a town?"

Rufe Houston's voice was high with scorn as he, and his two sons and Jace Fargo, halted at the edge of a cottonwood grove and looked upon Batesville — a solitary store building with accompanying structures.

"Told you it weren't much," Leo said. "Folks traveling stop here on account of there's a spring where they can water their horses and buy supplies at the store."

"I don't see no horses nowhere," Rufe muttered.

Jace pointed to the rear of the small, slanted-roof building that bore the sign RAMSEY'S GENERAL STORE across its front. "They's a barn out back. Wagon standing by the side. Like as not the horses are inside."

Rufe spat into the dust. "Well, if there ain't, we got us a mighty big problem," he said, and moving out from shade spread by the trees, headed across the open ground for the store.

It was well into the afternoon and the heat had faded somewhat. Birds were singing in the thickly leafed branches of the cottonwoods, and over where the spring had burst from the dark-red soil to form a pond, a duck quacked noisily.

They had made the flight from the arroyo below the prison without incident, encountering no one or seeing no one on their trail. He had completely fooled the warden and his guards, Rufe believed, and reckoned that it would be at least dark before a posse could be mounted — and by then it would be too late for them to start out.

When that hour came, he expected to be well on his way south, with plenty of miles separating him and his party from the area where a search would be going on. He would have been even farther if things had gone right and there'd been a horse waiting for him like they had it planned. But it was the same old story: depend on somebody else and you'll end up in the soup.

Maybe it was a lucky break, though — not the long, hot walk but the fact that they'd been forced to head west instead of south for the Mex border as he'd figured to do. The warden — Skerrit — and his posse would be expecting him to go north into the high mountain country, which was the direction cons usually took when they broke out. And there might be some of them who'd believe he would head for Mexico, but that was a slim possibility. The good part of it was that nobody'd look for him to go west; there was no safety that way, which in this instance made it the safest choice of all.

"You know this Ramsey?" Rufe asked. He was feeling better about it all, after giving it consideration, and while it had come about through no effort on his part, he was nevertheless congratulating himself on a fine bit of strategy.

Rufe had addressed the question to Leo, was continuing to ignore Billy as if he were not there.

"Not specially. Stopped by there a couple of times. Old man — kind of fat."

"He by hisself?"

Leo shrugged. "Got a woman — wife I reckon she is. Fat, too."

"Nobody else around — son, hired hand, somebody like that?"

"Ain't never seen nobody but him and the woman."

Rufe scrubbed at his bearded chin. "Good. I reckon this is going to be easy as shooting fish in a rain barrel."

He paused, glanced up. They had reached the landing that fronted the low, one-storied building. A squat, elderly man in overalls had appeared suddenly in the doorway. He held a leveled shotgun in his hands.

"What do you want?" he demanded.

Rufe's broad face reflected surprise. He looked around at his companions. "Now, ain't this a fine way for a man to welcome customers! Danged if I ever seen the likes of it before!"

"Customers!" Ramsey echoed. "You sure don't look like no customers to me. Them's prison duds you're wearing and them others with you ain't nothing but —"

"Now, I don't see what clothes has to do with a man spending his money," Rufe said. "Sure I got on duds I been wearing in the pen. Was let out a few days ago and ain't had time to fix myself up with a new outfit. Was hoping to buy myself the complete works here."

"Way I heard it the prison always gives a man a new suit and shoes when they turn him loose," Ramsey said, frowning. "How's it happen you ain't wearing them?"

"Could've had them if I'd wanted to hang around a couple more days. They didn't have nothing that'd fit me, and the tailor was sick with the flu. I plain was so danged glad my time was up that I couldn't wait."

"And we ain't nobody special, Mr. Ramsey," Jace Fargo said. "Just relatives of his'n — common folks come to meet him and go on west. We're hoping to get us a fresh start somewheres."

The storekeeper nodded, lowered his weapon, and stepped back. "I reckon you're all right," he said. "Being out here alone like I am, I have to be plenty careful who I let in my place."

"Sure can understand that," Rufe agreed as he stepped up onto the landing, crossed, and followed closely by his two sons and Fargo, entered the store.

"Hey — where's your horses?" Ramsey asked as if only realizing they had not been mounted. "Ain't natural for a man to be afoot in this country unless —"

"Unless what?" Rufe Houston snarled, and pivoting abruptly, seized the shotgun held by the storekeeper and wrenched it from his grasp.

Ramsey sagged back against the wall, his face chalk-white. "Nothing — nothing. What do you want?"

"Plenty — and we'll just help ourselves," Rufe replied, and unloading the shotgun, broke it in two over a nearby barrel.

He motioned to Fargo. "You know what we're needing in grub and such. Get busy and fill us up a couple of sacks. Better throw in a coffeepot and a spider, too, and some cups. And don't be forgetting blankets."

Jace Fargo nodded, moved off toward the counter at the back of the store and the shelves on the wall behind it where cans and boxes of food were neatly arranged. Halting, the outlaw rummaged about under the counter and came up with several flour sacks. Shaking one open, he began to fill it from the storekeeper's stock.

Rufe, in the process of strapping on a belted gun he had appropriated from a peg on the wall, turned his attention to Leo.

"Take your brother and go have a look-see in the barn for horses. Got to be some around here, somewhere."

Leo made no reply, simply beckoned to Billy, and together they dropped back to the store's entrance, recrossed the landing, and hurried off for the structure at the rear.

"Now," Rufe said to Ramsey, the holstered weapon now firmly resting against his thigh, "I reckon you and me can get down to business. Where you keeping your money? You got a cash box — or maybe a safe?"

The storekeeper, still slumped against the wall just inside the doorway, shook his head. "Ain't got neither one — and I ain't got no money."

Rufe Houston took a long, quick step forward. His big fist lashed out, caught Ramsey on the jaw, sent him to the floor. Before the man could stir, the outlaw reached down, grasped the front of his overalls in his thick fingers, and jerked him back onto his feet.

"You want to try answering my question again?" Rufe said in a mild tone. "I reckon you just didn't understand me. And this time you sure ought to tell the truth."

Ramsey's head wobbled loosely. "I ain't got no money," he mumbled. "Bought some new stock, took about all —"

"Where's your wife?" Rufe cut in, shaking the man savagely. "Maybe I can get her to do the talking."

"Ain't nothing — you can do — to her," Ramsey answered falteringly. "She died six months ago. . . . I'm telling you the truth, mister — I ain't got no money, leastwise nothing but a little change."

"How much is that?"

"Fifteen — twenty dollars maybe —"

"Where is it?"

"Got it here — in my pocket," Ramsey said, producing a handful of silver and currency.

Rufe Houston's fingers wrapped about the money, took it from the storekeeper. "Aim to have a good look around," he said, pocketing the cash, "and if I find more hid away somewheres you're going to be mighty sorry you lied to me."

"Ain't no more," Ramsey said wearily, rubbing his jaw. "Can look all you want, but you —"

"Pa," Leo called from the doorway.

Rufe turned to face his older son, now entering the store. "Yeh? You scare us up some horses?"

"Ain't but two. Looked good but there ain't no more. Counted six saddles, howsomever."

Rufe glanced at Ramsey. "You got some horses hid out in the brush?" he demanded harshly.

"No. Two's all there is —"

"Then what're you doing with all them saddles?"

"Took them in trade — folks coming by busted and needing groceries."

"Horses ain't much," Leo continued. "Do better pulling a wagon than with a saddle."

Rufe swore, spat on the floor. "Wagon's

too slow. We'll have to make them do so get them ready."

"We riding double?"

Rufe cursed again. "Now how the hell else you figure we can travel?" he said impatiently.

Leo shrugged, wheeled, and hurried back to the yard.

"You about done?" Rufe called then to Fargo as he crossed to a glass-topped case and helped himself to a generous handful of cigars.

"Reckon so," Jace replied. "Even scared us up a bottle of whiskey — was tucked away behind some boxes. I reckon the old codger's been sort of nipping on the side when his wife wasn't looking."

"Said she was dead," Rufe stated, shifting his gaze to the storekeeper. "You been lying to me about her?"

"No, she's dead all right," Ramsey said heavily. "Didn't like me drinking, so I kept a bottle hid out. Just sort of forgot about it after she passed on."

"You got another'n cached around here somewheres?" Jace asked.

"That's the only one —"

"Then I reckon we're ready to pull out," Fargo said, coming out from behind the counter. He had three of the flour sacks, all well filled, slung over his shoulders. "Got aplenty to get us to —"

"Arizona," Rufe supplied, and let his eyes settle on Ramsey. "What do you figure we best do with this bird? Sure don't want him telling somebody that we're headed west."

Fargo glanced to the front where Leo and Billy had appeared leading a pair of heavy-bodied horses. After a bit he shrugged.

"Well, he ain't give us no trouble. What say you just save that there bullet you was aiming to put in him if he'll promise to keep his mouth shut about us?"

"I'm afeard you're getting soft, partner," Rufe said, "but maybe you're right. . . . You giving me your word, old man?"

"I sure am!" Ramsey answered hurriedly. "I won't tell nobody you was here or where you was headed!"

"That's good," Rufe said, holstering his pistol. "And if you do I'll be hearing about it and the next time I'm by here I'll stop just long enough to blow your damned head off. Understand?"

"Yes — sir —"

"All right. . . . Let's go, partner. Maybe we can make a few miles on them nags the boys scared up before dark."

7

The first of the convicts were being marched in by the guards, several of them having been drafted into litter-bearers carrying the dead and wounded. The man in charge of the search party paused to report to Skerrit.

"They killed John Gurley," he said. "Joe Todd and Pete Aiken are in mighty bad shape, likely won't make it."

"Prisoners?"

"Percy Hayden's dead — shot right through the heart. Found him in that arroyo back of the rocks where them outlaws was waiting. Hud Jameson got his skull caved in and there's a couple of others got themselves bunged up a bit trying to get away. Rufe Houston was at the bottom of it, Warden. Had three friends waiting there in the rocks to help him make the break."

"You get him?"

"Nope — only one we haven't run down — him and his damned friends."

Ben Skerrit swore savagely under his breath. Rufe Houston had played him for a sucker. He'd put on the model-prisoner act for months, setting an example for the others in his cell block as well as for the men in general with his display of cooperation. It was evident now that it had all been part of a plan.

"I've got Clinton and Tolly Jones in the saddle looking for him. Told them to keep at it until they found him or it got too dark to search."

"This Houston — the one who started it — he give you trouble before?"

At the question Skerrit came about. It was Morrison, the governor's aide. Ben shook his head. "Took me in, completely," he said.

"Hell, old Rufe took us all in," the guard declared. "Don't go taking all the blame, Warden."

"I'm supposed to be smart enough not to be fooled by the likes of him," Skerrit said, anger tightening his voice as he wheeled to face another uniformed man hurrying up.

"We've got all the rest of the prisoners in their cells," the guard said.

Skerrit nodded crisply. "Keep them there until you hear different from me. Meantime, give these men a hand."

"You want them that tried getting away

thrown into solitary?"

The warden gave that brief thought. "Yeh — go ahead. It'll give them time to think a little."

Morrison waited until the guards had moved off and then, shrugging, said, "Too bad about this, Warden. Sure blows the governor's plans to blazes. He was figuring on a lot of favorable publicity to boost his chances next year."

Skerrit made no reply. At that moment he could care less about Burt Horn's political future. Houston was a dangerous killer and he was on the loose; he must be caught — tracked down — brought in at all costs.

At that moment he saw the sentries at the gates pause as they swung them closed to admit a woman and a young man. The wife — widow — of the slain guard, John Gurley, and their son, Dave. Skerrit took a step toward them, intending to express his condolences, but both looked away and hurried on to the infirmary.

"May as well forget that appropriation you were wanting the legislature to grant you for improvements," Morrison said. "When the news of this gets out — and you can depend on Tyler seeing to that — you'll be lucky if they don't cut your funds."

Skerrit was only half-listening. His thoughts were still on Houston — and on John Gurley's widow and son. They were blaming him for Gurley's death, indirectly of course, but putting it on him, nevertheless. He could imagine their accusatory words: "If you hadn't made it easy for the convicts, treated them soft, John Gurley would be alive."

Ben supposed there was some truth in it, and perhaps he was wrong in trying to help men who had gone wrong but who wanted to make amends. It was a difficult question to answer, but that was all beside the point now, and the man who had brought it all to a head — a killer who had been sent to the pen for life — was free.

"About forgot," Morrison continued. "Governor said to suggest that you get up a posse and go after the convicts that escaped."

"Only one got away, and guards — on horses — are looking for him now."

"He was a murderer — in for life, wasn't he?"

Skerrit only nodded, glanced around. Both gates were now secure, the prisoners were in their cells — except for the injured ones, who had been taken along with the two guards to the infirmary — and the yard was deserted except for a half a dozen of the uniformed men standing at their usual posts.

"What do you want me to tell the governor? You aim to just let your two mounted guards try to run down this Houston, or are you calling in the sheriff?" Henry Morrison's tone was impatient.

"Too late for the sheriff to do any good today," Ben replied. "Time we could get word to him in Capital City it'd be dark."

"Could start out at first light in the morning."

"What I figure. I'd like for you to take care of that for me when you and the rest get back to town. Tell him what happened and that I'll be obliged if he'll get right on it."

Morrison frowned, stared off toward the mess hall, from which Burt Horn and his party were emerging and moving toward them. Apparently, now that the yard had been cleared, they felt it safe to leave.

"Why don't you ride in and tell the sheriff?" Morrison asked. "Being the warden — it ought to be you."

Skerrit remained silent, waited until Horn and the others had reached them, evidently preferring to not go over the matter twice.

"I'm going after Rufe Houston myself,

Governor," he said, "if they don't bring him in within the hour."

Horn nodded, stared thoughtfully at the closed gates. "He the only one that got away?"

"The only one. He's a killer, was sent up for life. I can't let him run loose."

"You going alone?"

"Morrison's going to notify the sheriff for me when he gets back to town, ask him to mount a posse. But it'll be morning before he can get started. I can't afford to give Rufe Houston that much of a start."

Burt Horn rubbed at his jaw. "Not so sure it's a good idea — your going after him."

"Way I see it his escape was my fault," Skerrit said. "I put too much trust in him. Up to me now to bring him back before he can do any more killing."

"If he hasn't already," Tyler said dryly.

"That's possible," Skerrit admitted, hanging tight to his temper. He'd be glad when the newspaperman was gone. Never before had he met anyone who irritated him as much as Tyler did.

"You think it's wise for you to leave here at this time?" Horn asked, waving his party on toward the gates. They had earlier left their rigs just inside the prison's entrance.

"No problem," Skerrit said curtly. "Men have all settled down and the assistant warden can handle things."

Horn gave that thought while studying Skerrit's grim, angular face. "No idea of when you'll be back, of course —"

The warden's jaw tightened. "When I get that son of a bitch — can't tell you more than that."

Burt Horn shook his head slowly. "No need to warn you that you're an officer of the law. Houston's to be brought in alive."

"I'm making no promises," Skerrit said, and pivoting, strode off to his quarters.

True to his avowed intent, Ben Skerrit was within the hour riding through the prison gates and heading for the arroyos beyond the rocks where Rufe Houston and his outlaw friends were last seen.

He had ordered his horse, with a sack of trail grub and a canteen of water added to his saddle, when he called the assistant warden into his office and made known his plans. Now, wearing range clothing, belted gun on his hip, and feeling much as he did in the days when he was a lawman in pursuit of a wanted criminal, he was under way.

He encountered the two mounted guards shortly after pulling away from the towering stone walls of the prison. They told him that they had covered the near area in a wide circle but had failed to turn up any sign of Houston and his partners. They had searched carefully for hoofprints in the loose sand of the wash but none could be found — a fact that baffled them, for how could Rufe Houston and the others with him expect to escape without horses? They did find a few boot tracks, but they led to nowhere.

It wasn't logical, Skerrit admitted, but a man simply couldn't disappear from the face of the earth; Rufe and his friends had to be somewhere in the vicinity. He ordered the guards back to quarters, telling them to abandon the search, that the sheriff and a posse would be on the job that next morning, while he intended to do some looking around himself. The men, taking note of the firm, almost savage determination in his manner, nodded politely and continued on their way back to the prison.

That Houston's friends had come without horses to assist him in making an escape didn't make sense, Ben Skerrit thought as he watched the pair of uniformed men move off. It would seem normal for them to have left their animals somewhere nearby where they could quickly be reached; the guards, not trained to any extent in tracking, had simply overlooked the sign.

Skerrit reached the rocky outcropping where Houston's friends had lain in ambush, and halted. Considering the mass moodily for a bit, he headed the bay horse he was riding down into the shallow, ragged formation, allowed him to pick his way through, and came finally to the brush-lined, sand-floored arroyo. Immediately he saw a scuffed place on the sun-baked surface, reckoned that was where Rufe, or one of the outlaws with him, had killed Hayden.

There were many boot tracks along with the heel marks of Houston's heavy shoes all around the area where the luckless convict had fallen, but, strangely, Skerrit could see none going on up the wash that would lead, eventually, to the high mountain country. Skerrit turned his attention to the south, probed the sand with narrowed eyes. After a few moments he picked up a shallow indentation — a mark that looked as if it had been covered over and —

Ben's thoughts came to an abrupt stop and a tenseness began to build within him. The rasp of clothing against dry brush at the edge of the arroyo had reached him, set up a quick warning. It could be Houston and the other outlaws. Skerrit let his hand sink slowly until it rested on the butt of his pistol, turned quickly. A lean figure stepped into view, hands going up hastily. It was Dave Gurley, son of the guard who had been slain.

"What the hell's the matter with you, sneaking up on a man like that?" Skerrit demanded angrily. "And what are you doing here?"

Gurley, twenty years old or so, was of average height, wore ordinary cowhand garb, had a clean-shaven face, dark eyes and hair, and looked more like his mother than his father.

"Same thing you are, I reckon — looking for that bastard that killed my pa," he said coolly. "And I wasn't sneaking."

"Could've got yourself a bullet —"

"Maybe. I expect I'm as fast as you are with a pistol — probably even faster. Likely I would have got off the first shot, if it'd been necessary. You're out of practice, I'd bet."

"Don't take odds on it," Ben Skerrit said quietly. "How'd you know to come here?"

"One of the cons — a friend of Pa's — told me. Said he seen Houston and the others light out through here."

"He say who it was that shot your pa?"

Gurley's shoulders stirred. Close by in the brush insects were clacking noisily in the afternoon heat. "Nope, he didn't see who it was, but it was Rufe Houston. I know that for sure — he didn't like Pa."

"What makes you think there's something special about that? Convicts usually don't like guards."

"Pa said so once when he was home. A hell of a lot of things went on inside the walls that you never knew anything about, Warden. Your assistant, Hal Stewart, never let the word get past him to you. Molly-coddling them bastards the way —"

"Don't use that word around me!" Skerrit snapped, anger surging to the surface.

"I heard that the newspaper dude called it that, so it's the right word far as I'm concerned. Anyway, you making it soft for them convicts instead of treating them tough-like, you for sure caused Pa and the other guards plenty of trouble."

Dave's tone was resentful and filled with bitterness. Skerrit shrugged. "Go ahead, hang it on me if it'll make you feel any better. But I think, if your pa was alive, he'd tell you real quick that, overall, the system I used made his job a lot easier and safer."

"Sure wasn't very safe for Pa —"

"Was working fine until one bad apple spoiled it for everybody. . . . Wanted to tell you and your ma how sorry I was about John. When a man works in a prison, how-ever, he takes a risk — we all do. Your pa knew that same as all the other guards."

"Can't see that you're taking much of a chance, setting there inside your office. All you have to do is yell and a half a dozen guards with guns come running."

Skerrit's shoulders stirred indifferently again. He was neither in the mood nor had the time to argue with Gurley. Wheeling the bay around, he nodded crisply to the boy.

"I'll be obliged if you'll tell your ma how sorry I am about John when you get back to the house." The Gurleys lived, along with the families of other penitentiary employees, in a scatter of small structures outside the wall. "If it'll help any, can say I aim to bring in Rufe Houston, one way or another —"

"Best you tell her yourself," Dave cut in. "I ain't going home."

The warden paused, studied the younger man with faint suspicion. "Where're you going?"

"With you — after Houston."

Skerrit drew up stiffly on his saddle, his mouth set to a tight line. "No you're not. I've got no time to nursemaid you along."

"Nursemaid, hell! You won't be doing that — not by a damn sight! What you'll be doing is needing me."

Skerrit's smile was thin. "I sure can't

think of any reason for that."

"Tracking, that's why," Gurley said promptly. "Talked to them guards that were down here looking for sign. Said all they found was boot tracks — no hoofprints — and they lost them on down the wash a ways. You think you can find them and follow them to where they went, Warden?"

"Probably," Skerrit said. "Done my share of trailing while I was wearing a badge."

Dave Gurley frowned, surprised. "You a lawman once?"

"Was before the governor hired me on as the warden at the pen."

Gurley's shoulders came down. "Didn't know that," he said in a falling voice. "But I still figure I can help. I'm pretty good at tracking, if I do say so myself, and it's mighty important to me that Houston doesn't get away — same as it is to you."

Skerrit gave Gurley's words thought. Having the both of them working a trail would be much better, and faster, than if he went at it alone. And if Dave was as good as he claimed, both as a tracker and with the pistol he was wearing, it would be an advantage to have him along.

"All right," he said. "But we best get this

straight — I'm calling the shots. You do what I say, nothing more, and we stay together. I won't have you going off on your own."

"Sure," Dave said. "You're the boss."

"Something else — Houston belongs to me. Besides the murders he committed, he ruined a fine thing for a lot of men who were sincere in wanting to make themselves better."

"Which means you aim to kill him yourself when we find him for messing up your be-nice-to-the-convicts plan, and you don't want me horning in, that it?"

Ben Skerrit's set expression did not change. "Like I said, Houston's mine. That clear?"

"I savvy," Dave Gurley said, and turned back into the brush for his horse.

9

"Ain't that dust up there a piece?" Jace Fargo wondered aloud.

It was later afternoon and they had made good time despite the horses being forced to carry double. Such was due, likely, to the fact that both were big, strong animals accustomed to hard work, and while not fast, were untiring.

"Sure looks it," Rufe agreed. Leo was riding with him, leaving Billy to straddle Fargo's saddle skirt. "What do you say, son? Your eyes are younger'n mine."

"Dust for sure," Leo replied, squinting. "Looks like a wagon — one of them with a canvas top. Pilgrims, I expect, on the way to somewheres."

Rufe swore, pleased. "Now, that's just what we're wanting. Can get ourselves a couple more horses."

The pilgrim had two extra mounts tied to the rear of his wagon, they saw as they drew near. Again Rufe Houston swore happily.

"Better'n I'd figured," he said, grinning. "Can do some choosing. We best spread out. Jace, you swing around to his yonder side. Me and Leo'll come at him from the near. That way we'll box him in between us."

"What if he ain't of a mind to give up any of them horses?" Leo asked.

Rufe didn't look around, simply shrugged his thick shoulders. "What do you think you're wearing that gun for?" he replied, and then called out to the pilgrim. "Hey, mister, pull up!"

They had drawn ahead of the vehicle, an ordinary farm wagon that had been re-inforced in several vital places to make it more substantial for cross-country traveling. Canvas had been stretched over arching wooden bows to shelter the occupants from the sun. The team pulling the wagon, as well as the pair of spares following behind, was no better or no worse than the two animals taken from Ramsey.

"Where you headed?" Rufe, smiling, asked as he reined in close to the front wheel of the vehicle. Directly across Fargo and Billy had halted in a like position.

"Arizona," the man said warily.

He was a solid-looking individual with a stubble of beard, a gray-sprinkled mustache, and hard, coarse features. He had passed the lines to the team to his wife, a worn, listless woman, and now held a rifle in his hands. Evidently he had seen Houston and the others approaching and made ready.

"Arizona, eh? What's so good there that a man'd pull up stakes for?"

"Ain't knowing that — not yet. Just moving."

"I see. Get the itch myself now and then — me and my boys and my friend, there. It's just what we're doing right now — only we're heading for Texas. What'd you say your name was?"

"Name's Noah Waring — and I hadn't said it. This here's my wife, Cora. What's yours?"

"Smith — Charlie Smith. Young fellow behind me is my boy Leo. Friend there's named Jones and that's my boy Billy riding with him. Now we —"

There was movement behind Waring and his wife in the opening of the canvas arch. A face appeared — that of a girl, probably in her middle teens or a bit older.

"Pa forgot to mention me," she said with a smile. "I'm Jenny Waring."

Rufe swept off his hat in a grand gesture. "Why, howdy do, missy! You're a sight for sore eyes! How come you keep a pretty little thing like that all hid out, Waring?"

The pilgrim stirred angrily. "She's the

reason why we're having to move," he said. "You're a mighty lucky man having two sons. A girl ain't never nothing but trouble."

"Now, Pa, you know that ain't so," Jenny said in a chiding tone. "It ain't my fault the boys find me mighty fetching."

"Never mind," Waring snapped, glaring at Leo, who had dropped from his place behind Rufe and moved in for a closer look at the girl. "You get back in there and keep your mouth shut."

"Sure, Pa," Jenny said, and withdrawing at once, reappeared just as quickly at the rear of the wagon. Swinging her round hips, she swaggered up alongside Rufe.

"Jenny, you get back inside the wagon," Noah Waring ordered.

The girl, basking in the admiring appraisal of Houston and the others, shook her head impishly. "Don't fret, Pa, I'm just getting me a breath of air. It's hot in there."

She was well built if a little on the stocky side, had brown hair and eyes. The dress she wore fit tight, revealed the contours of her body, and accented a bosom much larger than could be expected of one so young.

"Whoo–oo–ee," Rufe said with a low

whistle. "Little lady, you sure are something!"

Jenny tossed her head and, arching her back, pivoted slowly. "I've been told that before — plenty of times."

"I'll just bet you have," Jace Fargo said, unable to remain silent any longer. "You —"

"Jenny! Get back in the wagon!" Waring's voice was stern, demanding.

The girl continued to ignore him and, moving past Leo, circled the team and halted beside Fargo and Billy. She centered her gaze on the youngest Houston.

"The cat got your tongue, boy? You ain't said one word about me. Don't you think I'm something, too?"

Billy pushed off Fargo's horse, dropped to the ground. "I sure do. It's just that I ain't seen nothing pretty as you in a long time, and it sort of took my breath away."

"Jenny!" Waring shouted, his voice reflecting alarm. "Get in the wagon. We're moving on."

"Now, just leave her be," Rufe said. "It's a mighty big treat having a little gal like that prancing around and showing herself off. Can't think it'd be much better unless she'd —"

"Jenny!" It was Cora Waring this time. "You mind your pa and get in this wagon!"

"She's all right, ma'am," Rufe said,

continuing to smile genially. "What she's doing won't hurt her none while me and your mister talk a little business."

"Business?" Noah Waring echoed. "What kind of business have we got to talk over?"

"Horses. Reckon you seen we was riding double."

Waring nodded. "Aimed to ask about that. You lose a couple?"

"Sure did, and we got a far piece to go. Need two real bad."

"Ain't selling," Waring said flatly. "We got a long ways to go, too, and we'll be needing —"

Rufe Houston's arm came up suddenly. The pistol in his hand jumped as a deafening blast shattered the quiet. As Jenny screamed in fright, Noah Waring half-rose from his seat, twisted slightly, and fell forward over the wagon's dash.

Cora Waring, holding a tight line on the startled, shying team, stared at Houston with shocked eyes. Abruptly she released the leather reins and snatched up the rifle that was slipping from her husband's stiffening fingers. Rufe triggered his pistol again. The woman jolted when the bullet smashed into her, and as Jenny screamed once more, fell back into the wagon.

With smoke coiling about him, Rufe calmly reloaded his weapon and slid it back into its holster. Raising his eyes, he glanced about at the expressionless faces of his two sons and Jace Fargo.

"Reckon that settles it far as horses go. Leo, you and your brother pick yourselves out the two best ones. Take a look inside the wagon see if the sodbuster had a saddle."

As Leo turned away, Rufe looked down at Jenny. The girl was gazing woodenly at the body of her father hanging half out of the wagon.

"Ain't but one saddle, Pa," Leo called from the rear of the wagon. "And it sure ain't much."

"Expect it'll have to do. You throw it on your horse. Billy'll have to ride bareback."

"What about the gal? We can't leave —"

"Nope, we sure can't, so pick out a horse for her, too. She'll come in right handy on cold nights."

10

"Can see right here where they climbed out of the wash," Dave Gurley said, pointing to faint scuff marks on the wall of the arroyo. "Was still afoot . . . I just can't figure them not having horses."

Skerrit nodded. "Looks like they tried wiping their tracks out with some brush," he said, raising his glance to stare out over the flat beyond the wash. And then in response to Gurley's comment, added, "Rufe wouldn't be that dumb. My hunch is they had horses tied up around here close, only they got loose and stampeded. Could've been a big cat — or maybe they were stolen — drifters or tramps."

"Make sense," Dave said, and spurring his mount up the side of the arroyo, began to study the ground. "They're heading west."

Skerrit probed his recollection of the country, frowned. "Old man Ramsey's place — Batesville. They're headed for there. We best get there fast — no telling what they'll do to him."

Ben roweled his horse, sent him lunging up the embankment and onto the flat. Not hesitating, the bay rushed on while Dave Gurley, raking his buckskin hard, hurried to swing in abreast.

They held the horses to a fast gallop until they reached the grove in which Ramsey's store stood. As they came to the edge of the clearing, Skerrit raised his hand and called a halt.

"Place looks quiet — almost deserted," he said. "Doubt if Rufe and his bunch are still around — but we ought to take it slow."

Dave Gurley made no reply. His face had suddenly grown hard and a glint had come into his eyes, changing him, lending him an older look. His hand had strayed to his pistol, now rested on its handle.

Skerrit shook his head. "I'm reminding you of what I said about Houston —"

Some of the tenseness seemed to fade from Gurley's taut shape. His hand fell away from the weapon at his side. His shoulders stirred. "All right," he murmured. "It's only that I've got to be sure — for Pa's sake. Taking him back alive to hang won't mean anything. He should've hung for that first killing he done, but he got off with life instead. Same thing'll happen again if —"

81

"You leave it to me," Houston said in a cold, promising voice. "This time Rufe will pay. . . . Now, I want you to circle left. I'll come in from the right. Watch yourself."

Dave pulled away at once, began to veer the buckskin toward the south end of Ramsey's store. Skerrit took an opposite course, and shortly they reached the ends of the porch fronting the structure and dismounted. Stepping up onto the wooden floor of the landing, the warden drew his pistol and listened. Gurley, motionless now at the opposite end of the porch, waited for Skerrit to signal.

From the trees near the spring doves were calling mournfully, and far back in the short hills beyond, a coyote yipped as if hoping to bring on night sooner. But within the store building all was quiet — too quiet, it seemed to Ben Skerrit. Reaching down, he deadened the jingle of his spurs with matchsticks and then, nodding to Gurley, crossed quickly to the door.

It was open. Removing his wide-brimmed hat, Skerrit peered inside. The place appeared orderly, undisturbed at first, and then he saw the broken sections of a shotgun near the wall to his right — and close by, the figure of the storekeeper.

"Ramsey," he called softly.

That the outlaws had been there was evident to Skerrit, but that they had gone was not so apparent. They could all be in the back of the store, hiding behind the counter or the wooden cases.

"Here," the storekeeper answered weakly. "Come on in."

"You alone?"

"If you're meaning them outlaws — yeh, they're gone."

Skerrit beckoned to Gurley, and stepping into the store, they crossed to where Ramsey was slumped on the floor, shoulders against the wall. He did not appear badly hurt, apparently had suffered several blows to the head that had stunned him. Ben, with Gurley's assistance, pulled the storekeeper upright and carried him to a rocking chair in the back of the cluttered room.

"Was it four men — one wearing prison clothes?" Skerrit asked as soon as Ramsey had been made comfortable.

The storekeeper rubbed at the side of his head carefully. "Yeh, was four of them. And one was a convict. Claimed he'd just been let out."

"They walking?" Gurley asked.

"Yeh," Ramsey said wearily. "I should've

figured they was bad ones — and I reckon I did when it come to me that they was afoot. Ain't nobody going afoot in this country unless they've had a accident or trouble of some kind. Was too late when I finally realized —"

"They get horses from you?" Skerrit cut in.

"Two — took my team and a couple of the saddles I done some trading for. Helped themselves to whatever else they wanted, too — grub, blankets, canteens — then robbed me of what money I had. . . . You mind looking in behind them sacks of salt, young fellow? There's a bottle of whiskey."

Gurley, stepping hurriedly in behind the counter, located the liquor and handed it to Ramsey. The man immediately pulled the cork with his teeth, spat it aside, and took a deep swallow from the bottle.

"Needed that," he said with a sigh, and offered the whiskey to Skerrit and Gurley, who both declined. "Was just too weak to get myself on my feet and go get it. Sure glad you two come along. You tracking that convict? He escape from the pen?"

"About noon," Skerrit replied. "How long ago were they here?"

Ramsey glanced through the window,

gave it a moment's thought. "Three hours, more or less. Kind of hard remembering —"

"If they got only two horses from you, then that means they were riding double when they left."

"Just what they was doing," Ramsey said, taking another pull at the bottle. The liquor was bringing him back to normal swiftly.

"You see which way they went?"

"Nope, I was laid out cold there on the floor. Big one — the convict — busted my shotgun in two, then knocked me out, near as I recollect. But I know which way they said they was going — west."

"West?" Skerrit repeated. "You sure about that?"

"Just what they said — west. I remember now they mentioned it a couple of times. Why? Ain't that what you figured they'd do?"

Skerrit shook his head. "Man running from the law usually heads for the mountains — north, or south for the Mexican border."

"My place is west, sort of, from the pen, and they come here —"

"One of them probably knew about you," Gurley said, "and they were looking for horses. You think they kept going west,

Warden?" he added, scrubbing at his jaw.

Ben Skerrit was gazing off through the open doorway. "Need to find some tracks to answer that — but my guess is they're headed for the border."

"South?" Ramsey said, coming erect in his chair. "I sure hope not!"

Ben looked at the man, puzzled. "What makes you say that?"

"It's the Waring family. Noah and his wife, Cora, and their girl. They passed by here this morning, going south. Sure would hate for them outlaws to catch up with them. Noah's got a couple of extra horses they'd be wanting — and that girl — Jenny, they call her — sure is something to look at. She's a bit forward, but she'd still have a mighty bad time of it if they got their hands on her."

"If that bunch rode south they'll for sure run into them," Skerrit said. "If they kept going west, then we've got nothing to worry about."

"I'll go have a look, see what I can find out," Gurley said, and pivoting, returned to the yard.

"Was real surprised to see the Warings moving on," Ramsey said. "Had a nice place about thirty miles from here. Been doing real good on it. Was the girl that caused them to pull stakes."

"The girl? How . . . ?"

"Reckon a man could say she was just too dang pretty for her own good. Was always a bunch of boys — and men, too — hanging around her, and she made the most of it, I was told. Flirted something fierce. Her folks couldn't do nothing with her.

"Now, I ain't saying she was bad, 'cause I plain don't know — was just told these things. But for Noah and his woman to just up and leave a good homestead, there has to be a reason. And from what Noah said to me when he was here this morning — I figure it was the girl. They was leaving the country, going somewhere where they wasn't known, and starting over. Jenny could change her ways and nobody'd —"

"They went south," Dave Gurley called from the landing. "Two horses loaded heavy. Tracks are plain as day — never took no trouble to hide them."

"Expect they figured that anybody asking would believe what they told Ramsey — that they were going on west," Skerrit said and glanced at the storekeeper. "You going to be all right?"

"Sure," the merchant said. "Don't worry none about me. I'm just hoping you can get to the Warings in time — before them outlaws do."

"Same here," Skerrit said in a grim voice, and wheeling, at a run rejoined Dave Gurley, waiting with the horses.

Billy Houston glanced at the sun, now lowering in the west. The horses were slow but they still had covered a good number of miles. Pa had said they'd ride till dark and then pull up for the night. They'd be in brushy hills by then where Jace Fargo said there'd be water and they could set up a good camp.

He hoped it would come soon. The girl, Jenny, was having a hard time of it riding bareback; she was continually sliding from side to side and all but fell off several times. On each occasion Pa and Leo both had invited her to sit in front of them on their saddles and ride double, but she had refused. She was plenty wise when it came to men, there was no doubt of that.

Pa hadn't changed, Billy had realized that from the beginning. He still favored Leo and treated him as if he were a hired hand with only a half a quart of good sense. And he'd not lost his yen for women, and after being locked up for all that time in the pen, his hunger for them would be worse than ever.

It was too bad the girl had to be in that sodbuster's wagon just as it was a fool thing for her to climb out and go strutting around showing herself off the way she had. More than likely her folks had warned her to stay out of sight when they saw Pa and him and the others coming, but it was plain Jenny did just as she damn well pleased.

Well, she'd pay for it that night. She'd probably wish she'd listened to her folks and kept under cover. Even if matters had gone as they had — Pa killing that man and his woman — Jenny could have hid out until Pa and him and the others had gone and then taken one of the horses and ridden back to that general store, Ramsey's.

But there was no sense in hashing it over now. It was done; the pilgrim and his wife were dead, which sure didn't seem to bother Jenny much; and they were all on the way to the Mexican border.

The girl had done some bawling right after it happened — not for her pa, it seemed, but for her ma. All in all, he'd say their deaths didn't hit her very hard. Billy reckoned it would be the same with him if Pa got killed. It might cut him a little bit, but he sure as hell wouldn't shed any tears. Chances were he'd have a feeling of relief.

If Leo got himself plugged and cashed in, it might be a little different, but not much. Leo wasn't so bad when he wasn't around Pa, but let them get together and Leo, like that lizard somebody once told him about, would change completely and become another fellow — a duplicate of Pa.

It never occurred to Billy to just cut loose from Pa and Leo and take off on his own. It had always been the three of them ever since Ma had died — he'd been about ten at the time. They'd knocked around together, working on some ranch if it suited Pa's purpose, or maybe they'd just loaf about some town while he lined up a robbery — or the law ran them out.

He'd taken part in his first holdup at the ripe old age of twelve, being on the sidelines prior to that as the horse-holder. After he had become a full partner, he'd done his share, never shirking when it was necessary to use a gun or to stand on his own when it came down to shooting it out with the law.

But Pa having been away for so long, and having changed none, and Jace Fargo coming in as a full partner in the family was stirring Billy's mind to new and deeper thoughts.

Why stick with Pa and Leo — and Fargo? He'd never been given a fair share when it came to splitting up the take from a holdup or robbery, anyway, and now, with Fargo in on the deal, he'd probably get even less — so why put up with it?

Why not shove off on his own? He sure'n hell couldn't be any worse off, and he wouldn't have to put up with Pa and Leo any longer.

Jenny was glad her pa was dead, that she was finally free of him, once and for all. He had been a mean, cruel man, all too often brutal. In her younger years she had feared him, but by the time she had reached fifteen she had come to accept his treatment as a fact of life and fear had vanished.

Usually his punishment was administered with the flat of his broad hand, but later he'd brought into use a length of harness strap. It had hurt considerably more and on occasions left red welts, but at such times Jenny had not once cried, thus refusing him the satisfaction of seeing her in tears.

Most often Noah Waring's castigations stemmed from some incident concerning older boys and men — a circumstance she had little control over, she believed, just as the clover blossoms in the field back of their house just naturally attracted bees. It was simply nature at work.

But it infuriated Waring, and he did his best to keep her away from the opposite sex until she reached what he considered the marrying age or had met a man suitable to him as a husband for her. As a result a great deal of clandestine activity took place in secluded areas on the homestead that Noah Waring was never aware of — a fact that Jenny took a great deal of satisfaction from.

Not that Jenny was a bad girl. She was simply frivolous, reckless, and constantly treading on dangerous ground, and that, plus the violent opposition of her father, made it a heady game that did much to relieve the monotony of everyday life on a farm.

But Jenny reckoned she was in for it this time. She'd overplayed her hand and no doubt was in deep trouble. That the men who had grabbed her — at least, three of them — were hard-case killers, was apparent. And she guessed that was especially true of the old one in the prison clothes who'd shot her pa and ma. But she reckoned she could take care of herself. She'd only been outmaneuvered once, and that was by a pots-and-pans drummer who'd come by the house when she happened to be there alone. She'd learned a lot from him about men and that was going to stand her in good stead now, just as had been some advice given to her by her ma, who walked in on them.

Poor ma . . . she was out of her misery. Her life had been nothing but one of slavery — years during which she had been in total fear of Noah Waring and his cruelty. Jenny guessed the worst beating she'd ever taken from him was the time she had interfered when he'd taken his fists to Ma. It had all started over some trivial incident that amounted to very little, but as was Noah Waring's nature, it had sent him into a blind, ungovernable rage.

Waring had turned his fury from his wife to Jenny when the girl had leaped upon his back and began pummeling him; he had thrown her clear and knocked her almost senseless when she struck the wall of the room they were in.

He had used his rock-hard fists on her that time, leaving her in such condition that she was hardly able to get around for several days. But the pain had brought some satisfaction to her; at least her ma had been spared for that one time. Thinking about it, she reckoned the outlaw who had killed her pa had actually done the world a favor, for no man as mean as he was deserved to live.

But Jenny Waring realized that the outlaws would be doing her no favors. They would expect her to be at their beck and call for any purpose at all times and, like her pa, would brook no disobedience.

She had always dreamed of freedom, of the day when she would leave the homestead and get far away from her parents. The circumstances didn't matter, whether she was on her own or with a husband, which was the least desirable; what did count would be that she was at last free of a life she had come to despise.

Now such was at hand. It was not just as she would prefer it to be, but she was out on her own with no one such as Noah Waring to exercise authority over her. The humdrum existence that had weighed so heavily on her shoulders and bored her to utter distraction was behind her, a thing of the past. She was free — free to do as she damn well pleased.

Almost . . . The first big step had been taken, or rather, thrust upon her, thanks to the outlaw one of the men called Rufe and the two younger ones addressed as Pa. She was not letting herself think about the murders that had been committed; there was nothing to be gained. What she must consider was the new world that had been opened up to her.

Jenny was smart enough to know that her situation, until she could get away from the outlaws, was going to be far from pleasant. She'd weathered some rough times in the past, however, and for the sake of the future, she'd survive.

The clever thing to do would be to pick out one of the outlaws, make herself his woman. In that way maybe she'd not be forced into belonging to all of them.

Jenny glanced at the men riding abreast to either side of her. Rufe — Jace — the one with the sneer on his dark face, Leo — and the youngest of the four, Billy. She let her gaze rest on him. He didn't seem as mean — she guessed the right word was *evil* — as the others. She'd line up with him and make the best of it until an opportunity came to escape.

12

"It's a wagon," Dave Gurley said, shading his eyes from the last slanting rays of the lowering sun. "One of them with a white-canvas top — like pilgrims crossing the country use."

"It stopped?" Skerrit asked, endeavoring to make out the distant object. He had better-than-average sight, but was forced to admit that Gurley's powers of vision were astounding — on par with his ability to track.

"Yeh, seems. Can't see nobody moving about. Either they've pulled up to rest the horses, or there ain't nobody alive."

The warden nodded soberly. Dave's latter observation could be true. Rufe Houston had already shown his contempt for life, and the men riding with him undoubtedly were of similar nature.

"Let's get down there," Ben said, suddenly brusque. "I've got a hunch we're already too late."

"Same here," Gurley said, and spurred his horse.

A short time later as they rode out of a stand of cedars, Skerrit lifted a cautioning hand, and slowed. Gurley veered in beside him. Hands resting on their weapons, they considered the apparently deserted wagon, now less than a hundred yards away.

"Still can't see nobody," Dave commented. "It's getting a mite dark, however. Maybe we'll find somebody on the other side."

"Or inside," Skerrit added. "What bothers me is all I can see is one horse — and there's supposed to be four if it's the family Ramsey was telling us about. You see the others?"

"Nope. Could be in that brush over to the right." Gurley paused, tipped his hat farther over his eyes for additional protection from the sun. "Could be something else in that brush, too — Rufe and his friends, just waiting for us to come in close."

"That come to me, too," Ben said. "Let's circle around to the right of the wagon, come in on its blind side. I'm pretty certain there's nobody around, but I'm not fool enough to take a chance on it — not where Rufe Houston's concerned."

Side by side, hands riding the butts of their pistols, Skerrit and Dave swung wide and approached the vehicle, standing silent and forsaken in the fading sunlight. Abruptly Gurley spoke.

"They're dead — man and a woman. Can see them. And there ain't but one horse."

Still cautious, Skerrit nodded grimly and continued. His attention now was focused intently on the stand of brush beyond the wagon. Rufe and his bunch could be there — waiting in ambush. There was no way of knowing just how far ahead of them the outlaws had been. That they had been the ones to attack the Warings, he recalled Ramsey had named them, was a near certainty, and the delay that would have incurred in doing so could have made it possible for Dave Gurley and him to catch up.

Abruptly Gurley drew his pistol and spurred toward the brush. Reaching it, he veered sharply, circled, and then, reappearing, returned at an equally fast run.

"Ain't nobody hiding in there," he said, holstering his weapon. "Looks like they killed that homesteader and his wife and then made off with three of the horses."

Skerrit, cold anger flowing through him at the thought of what Rufe Houston had done, along with the realization that he, indirectly, was responsible, moved in closer to the wagon. Waring was doubled forward over the dashboard. His wife lay across the back of the seat, the upper part of her body inside the canvas arch.

"Damn those bastards to hell," Dave Gurley muttered from nearby. "Was no call for this. Them folks couldn't've give them any trouble."

"Probably refused to let them have the horses they needed —"

"That don't add up. Why'd they take just one? They was riding double — would need two —"

"Ramsey said the Warings had two extra horses," Skerrit reminded. "Take a look inside, see if the girl's in there. If not, you've got the answer."

"I'd forgot about her," Dave said, and dropped from his saddle. Circling to the rear of the vehicle, he climbed aboard. After a few moments he reappeared.

"She ain't in here, Warden. Looked good under everything. Ain't nothing but clothes and bedding, things like that."

"Means they took her with them. Explains why they rode on with a third horse."

"Don't look like they bothered with anything else," Gurley said, glancing around.

"Rufe and them weren't interested in anything but horses — and the girl. Expect we'd better find a couple of shovels and bury these people."

Dave nodded soberly, turned, and started again for the rear of the vehicle. "Seen some tools inside. I'll fetch a couple of blankets, too." He paused, looked directly at Skerrit. "What about the girl? If they've got her, which I reckon they have, hadn't we best keep going and try to catch up?"

Ben gave that thought, finally shrugged. Stepping up to the wagon, he lifted Cora Waring's body from the seat and moved off to the side of the trail.

"They're three, maybe four hours ahead of us. Not a chance of overtaking them before dark," he said, laying the woman down on the cooling sand. "We'd be too late to stop anything — even if we could find them without being spotted."

He started to also say that Jenny Waring, judging from what Ramsey had told him, could more than likely take care of herself, but let it pass since it had come to him as gossip and not worthy of repeating.

"Yeh," Gurley said, "reckon you're right," and moving on, reentered the wagon. Rummaging about, he came up with two spades. Tossing them out the front, he then pulled blankets from the pallet on the floor and returned to the outside. As he came up, Skerrit was laying the body of Noah Waring beside that of his wife. Both had been shot at close range by a heavy-caliber weapon — probably a forty-five.

Wordless, each man then took up one of the spades, and working together, they dug a grave large enough to hold both of the Warings. That done, they wrapped the bodies separately and then laid them side by side in the trench. When the grave had been filled and mounded, Gurley tossed his tool aside.

"They'll be needing a marker," he said, his voice barely controlled as he moved toward the wagon. "Seen some pieces of wood inside. Can fashion a cross."

"Go ahead," Skerrit replied, his hatred for Rufe Houston now a sullen force within him. Wheeling abruptly, he glanced to the west. The sun had now set behind the ragged horizon of hills and darkness was beginning to close in. Taut, he looked about for another chore, for something that would relieve the anger within him.

"I'll turn Waring's horse loose so's he can feed," he said, and crossing to where the animal stood head down and still in harness, began to free it.

He felt some better when that was done

and turned then to preparing an evening meal. It was full night by the time he had accomplished that and Dave Gurley had finished the marker. Now, sitting by a low fire eating fried meat, warmed-over bread, and drinking strong, black coffee, Skerrit considered what they had best do next.

"Be tough trying to track out there," Gurley said when the warden had broached the possibility. "There's a good moon, but the ground's hard and plenty rocky in places. Could easy lose a trail even if I could find it."

"Not worth the risk," Skerrit said. "Horses can use the rest, anyway. And like as not Rufe and his bunch are in the same shape. Horses they're riding have been on the run all afternoon. Means they'll pull up till morning, too."

"I'm worrying some about that girl —"

"Wish we could help her," Skerrit said, taking a sip of the steaming coffee. A chill had set in soon after the last of the sun's glow had died in the sky, and the fire felt good.

"Heard some of what that storekeeper said about her. Guess she ain't exactly no babe in the woods when it comes to men."

"I'm not putting much stock in what Ramsey said. Probably be better for her if she is that way, but we can't be sure. Anyway, you might as well know where I stand on that — she's second in line in my mind."

"And Rufe Houston's first, that it?"

"Right. He's what's important to me and I won't take a chance on losing his trail out there in the dark — not for her or for anybody else. That may be a cold way to look at it, but . . ."

Gurley let the moments run past, then, "But?" he prompted.

In the reddish glow of the fire Ben Skerrit's features appeared sharp, chiseled. "Houston's the only thing in my life — and that won't change until I get him in my sights and gun him down," he said quietly.

Dave smiled tautly. "My sentiments, exactly," he said, and glanced up at the star-filled sky. Dropping his gaze, he let it rest on the horses, picketed nearby.

"Was a half a sack of oats in the wagon. I gave some to the animals. What're we doing with that horse of Waring's? Taking him along'll slow us down plenty."

"We leave him," Skerrit said. "Can fend for himself. Can put out what feed there's left, and knock the head in of that water barrel so he can drink."

"Somebody'll probably come along, claim him."

"Most likely," Ben said, staring off to the south where several wolves were howling into the night. Setting his cup aside, he yawned, stretched. "I'm ready for a little sleep."

"Same here," Gurley said, rising. "Pretty good bed in that wagon. You got anything against using it?"

"Not a thing," Skerrit said, also coming to his feet. "Let's go."

13

"Jace, you sure there's a spring back up in them hills?" Rufe asked, taking a swallow from the bottle of whiskey.

It was late in the day. Following Fargo's directions, they had cut off the trail to the south and were now bearing due east for a line of low, brushy round-tops.

"Said there was, didn't I?" Jace demanded peevishly. He'd answered the same question a half a dozen times in the past hour, but Rufe, pretty well liquored up, seemed not to remember.

"All right, all right, was just asking," Rufe said placatingly, with a wave of his hand. "It just don't look like country where there'd be water."

"It's there," Fargo reassured him. He had drunk his share from the bottle of whiskey they'd taken from Ramsey, too, but it showed on him only in the thickness of his tongue. "Holed up there a many a time in the last couple of year. Just keep your shirt on. We'll be getting there pretty soon."

"I'm hoping so," Rufe said, " 'cause I'm getting powerful hungry. Hell, I ain't eat all day — 'cepting early this morning." He paused and, swaying unsteadily on the saddle, turned his flushed face to Jenny Waring. "You cook good, girl?"

"Good enough for you," she snapped.

Rufe grinned, glanced about at the others. "Real hard mouth, ain't she? Well, I reckon I can cure her of that."

"She sure got over her pa and ma quick," Jace observed as the horses, reaching the first of the hills, began a slow climb. "I'll bet she was a loving daughter!"

Rufe helped himself to another pull at the near-empty bottle, passed it to Fargo. Jace downed a swallow, returned it.

"What about it, girl?" Rufe asked. "You a good, loving daughter?"

"Not so's you'd notice," Jenny replied coldly. "I was glad to see my pa dead. Would've killed him myself someday if you hadn't come along and done it for me."

Rufe laughed. "Well, now! Seems we got us a regular little hellcat, boys! What about your ma, girl? You glad she's dead, too."

"I sure as hell am — but not for the same reason," Jenny said. "She was living a dog's life — worse — with him. Ma's better off out of it. Maybe she'll get some rest now."

"It sure don't look like you suffered none," Leo said, eyeing her admiringly.

"I look out for myself," the girl said flatly, "and I intend going right on doing it. And while we're talking, I'm warning you — especially you, Grandpa," she added, pointing a finger at Rufe, "you ain't caught yourself no little dove, so don't go thinking you've got —"

"Grandpa!" Rufe snorted, the word finally penetrated his dulled senses. "Damn you! I'll show you who's a grandpa!"

"Doubt that," Jenny said quietly. "I ain't standing for no wrassling around — not from any of you. Try it and you'll be wishing you'd never took the idea."

"My, my," Leo said chidingly, "you sure are a mean one, ain't you? Well, I bet I can —"

"You ain't doing nothing, boy!" Rufe broke in harshly. "She belongs to me — rightful. Was me that got rid of her pa and ma, and was me that took her. Now, I'm sure figuring on my reward. I been cooped up in the pen for so long I've dang nigh forgot what a woman looks like."

"Well, you've seen me," Jenny stated flatly, "and that's far as it goes. I'll do your cooking, but that's all. I ain't nobody's woman — nobody's! Best you all get that straight!"

When she finished speaking, Jenny Waring was staring directly at Billy. There was a slight smile on her lips as if she were excepting him from the pronouncement and wanted him to know it.

Anger had begun to glow in Rufe Houston's eyes. "We'll just see about that, missy!" he shouted. "Soon as we get to that damned spring and pull up, me and you's going to do some talking — alone. . . . Jace, where the hell's that damn spring? Jace!"

Fargo, dozing, jerked himself upright on his saddle. He considered the surrounding country through watery eyes, pointed ahead.

"Right on a ways," he said. "Them rocks — that's where the spring is."

"About time," Rufe grumbled, having another drink from the almost-empty bottle. "Sure are needing some more liquor. Jace, there any place around where we can get us another bottle?"

Fargo pointed indefinitely toward the east as the horses plodded wearily across a narrow flat. "Town on that way a piece. Called Haystack. Can get whatever we want there — whiskey, grub, women, gambling —"

"That sounds mighty inviting," Rufe said, wiping at his mouth with the back of a hand. "We can do some resting here for the night, then pay us a visit to this here Haystack place."

"You figure we ought, Pa?" Leo said at once, glancing back over his shoulder. "Like as not we're being trailed by them guards from the pen, or maybe a sheriff's posse."

"The boy's right," Fargo said. "They ain't just letting us go."

Rufe wagged his head. "Hell, they ain't following us — leastwise they ain't on our trail." His words were slow, thick. "Ain't saying they ain't doing some looking, but we throwed them off our trail back there at that arroyo. I'll bet the posse's working north, thinking we headed into the mountains — if they got one mounted."

"Maybe," Fargo said skeptically. "But I ain't for taking no chances. My neck's in this now, too — us killing a couple of them screws and that convict, and then you plugging them sodbusters. I say we spend the night here, then move on —"

Rufe gave that thought. His broad face was flushed and shining with sweat. His mouth sagged and there was an unsteadiness to him while his eyes had assumed a dullness.

"Want you all to get this straight," he

said finally. "I'm bossing this here she-bang, and it'll be me saying what we'll do!"

"Sure, Pa," Leo said, coming to Fargo's aid. He winked at Jace meaningfully. "Like you said before, it ain't smart to take chances, especially with all that gold waiting for us down in Mexico. We'll pull up and camp at that spring, then move out at first light in the morning."

Rufe frowned, his befuddled senses not grasping the situation fully. After a bit he nodded.

"Just what I was saying — we ain't taking no chances. Want you to keep remembering that —"

"There's the spring," Fargo cut in. "Best camping place is on the yonder side."

The horses, smelling the water, quickened their pace eagerly, and shortly the party, circling the small pond created by the spring, halted on its south side in a small clearing and dismounted.

Rufe, coming slowly about, clung to the saddle horn to steady himself. Denied liquor, except on rare, stolen occasions, during all those months inside the penitentiary, his system had grown unaccustomed to its effect and he was now almost off his feet from the quantity of whiskey he'd consumed.

"Billy, you help the gal rustle up a bite to

eat," he ordered, speaking with effort. "I'm going to set down there by the water, take me a little nap till it's ready."

"Reckon I'll be doing the same," Jace Fargo added. He was only a little better off than Houston. "One of you boys better look after the horses."

Billy was standing near Jenny. She smiled at him, but he turned away without comment and, moving off into the brush, began to collect wood for a fire.

"Here's the grub," Leo said, taking the bulging flour sacks that were hung across Fargo's saddle and dropping them at the girl's feet. "Expect you'll find everything you'll be needing."

Jenny nodded. Taking up the sacks, she moved to the center of the clearing where a previous pilgrim had arranged a number of rocks into a cooking pit. Setting the sacks close by, she began to open them.

Leo stood for a time watching her, taking in her every move and obviously admiring what he saw. Then, gathering up the reins of the worn horses, their thirsts now satisfied, he picketed them nearby, where they could graze on the thin grass.

Billy, arms loaded with wood, returned to the camp and, dropping the supply close to the pit, began to take up sticks, break them to proper length, and lay them in the hollow between the rocks. Jenny, skillet in one hand, paused, glanced at him.

"You're not like them others," she said in a low, almost-hopeful voice. "I seen that back at the wagon."

Billy shrugged, continued to prepare for the fire.

"I'm praying that you'll be my friend," the girl said. "Maybe I talk kind of hard, but I'm scared down deep."

"Pa's pretty rough, all right," Billy admitted, shifting his attention to Rufe, who, in concert with Jace Fargo, was snoring noisily.

"I reckon he ain't no rougher'n me," Leo cut in, coming up from behind them. "And him being in the shape he's in, I reckon that makes you my woman — leastwise while he's sleeping." Reaching down, Leo grasped the girl by the wrist and jerked her to her feet. "Come on, you and me are taking a little walk, and you ain't going to say nothing to Pa about it, either — understand?"

"Let go of her!" Billy yelled, knocking his brother's hand clear as he lunged upright. "You ain't doing nothing to her!"

Leo's head thrust forward and his eyes narrowed. "You stay the hell out of this, boy," he said, imitating Rufe as near as possible. "You get to fixing us a meal like Pa said. Me and Jenny'll be busy for a bit."

Billy rocked forward, snatched up a fair-sized length of wood. "You back off, Leo," he ordered in a cold voice. "I'm warning you right now — you leave her alone or I'll knock your damn head off!"

Leo frowned, dropped back a step. Jenny moved hurriedly away from him and took up a stand behind the younger Houston.

"You forgetting who you are, boy?" Leo asked, still aping Rufe.

Billy started to speak, but Jenny's words came first. "Nope, he's just remembering he's a man. Now, get away from us so's we can get our chores done — and you best stay away! Billy means just what he said."

14

Billy Houston spent the night at the mouth of a hollow in the rocks where Jenny Waring had lain down to sleep. Shoulders against the flat of a large boulder, he had alternately dozed and awakened, his one thought in mind being to keep Leo away from the girl.

In his own mind he wasn't exactly certain of why he had assumed the role of her protector. In times past he would have simply ignored the situation and allowed his brother to do as he pleased. The same applied when it came to Rufe; he would have considered it none of his business and kept out of the way — partly because that actually was the truth of it and partly out of fear of his pa's heavy and all-too-ready hand.

Now, as he lay, chilled and uncomfortable, staring at Rufe and Jace, still wrapped in a drunken sleep at the edge of the clearing, and at Leo, rolled in a blanket nearby, he was having second thoughts.

Why the hell had he stood up for Jenny

Waring? She meant nothing to him. There'd been times in the past when Leo or his pa had roughed up some girl or woman, and it hadn't occurred to him to interfere. There'd even been a few times when he'd taken a hand in such; so why, for hell's sake, had he stepped in and prevented Leo from having his way with Jenny?

He sure had no special feeling for her — no big yen. He could think of a dozen girls he'd met who were better-looking than she — and who'd welcome his attentions. Why Jenny?

Billy stirred, dug into his pocket for tobacco and papers, and rolled himself a cigarette. He didn't care much for smoking — considered it a nuisance, in fact — but there were moments when he was puzzled or disturbed and smoke in his lungs eased his nerves, made him think more clearly.

Pa would be waking up pretty soon, he guessed. Rufe had slept the entire night almost without moving, the liquor and weariness combining to throw him into a deathlike torpor. Fargo, too, had fallen into a deep coma, but he did move now and then and mutter between snoring.

Billy reckoned he'd better get things ready for his pa — the others didn't particularly matter. He'd as soon have no trouble with Rufe, who was going to be furious anyway when he woke up and realized he'd passed the night without fulfilling the plans he'd had for Jenny. If a meal was ready and the horses all set to ride out, it was possible that his pa's disposition might improve a bit.

Crossing to the pit, Billy collected some of the dry wood he'd carried in the night before and, piling it in the blackened cavity, set it afire. He went then to the hollow in the rocks where Jenny lay sleeping and shook her vigorously. She sat up immediately, eyes wide and questioning.

"Want you to get something to cooking," he said in a low voice. "Aim to have everything ready for Pa so's he can eat and then ride out."

Jenny nodded her understanding and, shivering from the cold, threw her blanket aside and got to her feet. She was fully dressed, even to the high-top shoes she was wearing, and as Billy turned away, she laid a hand on his arm and halted him.

"Never got a chance to thank you for last night — for keeping your brother away from me, I mean. Why'd you do it?"

Billy rubbed at his jaw. "Been asking myself the same question," he replied, and moved on.

Crossing the clearing, he paused to drop more fuel on the fire and then stepped up beside Leo, still sleeping soundly. Nudging his brother with a toe, he roused him.

Leo, face angry, glared at him. "What the hell you want?"

"Get up," Billy ordered. "Horses have to be saddled so's they'll be ready to ride out."

"Your job," Leo said, and turned over.

Billy bent over, grasped the blanket his brother had wrapped about himself, and jerked it clear. Leo cursed wildly, scrambled to his feet. Eyes blazing, he confronted Billy.

"Just who the hell you think you are?" he demanded. "I took that off you last night when you got in my way — and I ain't yet figured out why I did. But it ain't going to happen again! I'll beat your damn head off —"

"You want me to tell Pa what you was aiming to do?" Billy cut in quietly.

Leo drew back, threw a quick glance at Rufe, now awakening. "You do and I'll sure'n hell fix you good!" he warned.

"What the devil's going on? What's all that ruckus?" Rufe shouted angrily.

Billy glanced at his brother, said, "Ain't nothing, Pa. Was telling Leo we best get

118

the horses ready because you'll be wanting to move out soon's you eat."

Rufe scrubbed at his whisker-covered face with one hand, shook Fargo awake with the other. He gave Jenny, working over the fire, a brief glance, and nodded.

"Yeh, that's right. Figure to move right out. You boys get busy."

Billy turned, headed for the tethered horses. Reaching them, he began to throw gear on the nearest. At that moment Leo stepped up behind him.

"I can't savvy what's got into you, boy," he began.

"Name's Billy. Use it."

Leo swore. "That's what I'm meaning. You all of a sudden like've got the idea you're mighty tough. Pa'll take that out of you plenty damn quick if you —"

"That'll be Pa's business — and between him and me," Billy stated flatly, finishing with the horse. "When it comes to me an' you, that's something else."

"What's that mean?"

"This — you ain't Pa, and I ain't taking no sass off you no more. Goes for giving me orders, too. You ain't nothing more'n me, Leo!"

"You figure you can back that up?"

"Yes, sir — any damn time you say! With

fists, clubs, or pistols, I ain't caring which! You name it!"

Leo shook his head, perplexed, as Billy moved to the second horse, began to prepare it. "Just can't figure out what's come over you," he said, repeating himself.

Billy paused, looked off to the east, where the sun was beginning to break over the horizon. "I ain't sure myself, but it's happened," he said, and stepped back. "I done my share here. You finish up. I'm going back and see if the coffee's ready."

Wheeling, Billy returned to the clearing. Rufe and Jace were now hunched near the fire, tin cups of steaming, black coffee in their hands, bloodshot eyes on Jenny as she went about her duties. Billy wondered what his Pa had said to the girl about the previous night, or if pride had kept him from saying anything. Rufe would feel that he'd failed where she was concerned, and that realization would be hard for him to swallow.

"How long'll it take us to reach this here town — whatever you called it?" Rufe asked.

Fargo took a sip of his coffee, then stared gloomily into the cup. "Some whiskey in this'd sure help out a lot," he muttered. "It'll take most all day forking them old plow horses."

"Hadn't been for Billy we'd been riding some good horses," Rufe said sourly, and put his gaze on Jenny. "You about got some vittles ready, girl?"

She looked up from the skillet. "You can eat right now if you like your meat raw," she answered. "Else you'll have to wait a bit longer."

Rufe spat, tossed the remainder of his coffee against the rocks surrounding the fire pit. "Well, I'm hoping your grub's better'n your coffee. This ain't nothing but rainwater."

"Then you best boil it up yourself, Grandpa," Jenny said icily.

Rufe Houston's eyes narrowed. "I've had about enough of your lip, girl. I aim to take a bit of that out of you."

Jenny laughed. "Seems I recollect you saying that about last night."

Billy shot a quick look at the girl, caught her attention, and shook his head warningly. She was making a big mistake badgering Rufe, and he wished she would realize that. He could remember a time or two before Rufe had gone to prison that he'd lost his temper and the people involved ended up taking a terrible beating.

"She's just a-funning, Pa," he said,

hoping to smooth over the threatened turbulence.

"Funning — hell!" Rufe shouted. "I'll show her who's funning! Them horses ready?"

"Expect so. Leo was finishing up —"

"Leo? Why the hell ain't you doing it?"

"Because I've done my share. Up to Leo to do his."

Rufe stared at his younger son suspiciously. "You're acting mighty smart, boy, real uppity-like. I'm going to have to straighten you out a mite, too."

Fargo laid a hand on Rufe's arm. "Let it go for now, Rufe. If we're going to Haystack, we ought to get started. Just thinking about it's sort of stirred me up — all the women and good whiskey and such. You can take care of him — her, too — later."

Rufe considered that dourly. Then, "Yeh, guess you're right. Dish up that grub, girl, so's we can pull out."

15

The morning was clear and cold. Gurley built a fire and stood, backside to it, chafing his hands and shivering while he warmed himself and watched Ben Skerrit get the necessary items together for a meal. After a time he glanced off to the south.

"I'll take a look around, see for certain which way that bunch went when they left here," he said, and moved off.

He and Dave had gotten along much better than expected, Skerrit thought as he watched the younger man walk away. The hostility Gurley had exhibited toward him in the beginning had softened, and there was now a cool sort of friendship, or perhaps it was better called respect. Whatever, Skerrit was pleased with the change of attitude, and he hoped nothing would happen to alter it when they caught up to Rufe Houston.

Setting the pot of water over the flames to heat for coffee, Ben sliced chunks of salt pork into a frying pan and placed it on the fire also. Then, removing the skins and quartering two of several potatoes he had buried in the ashes of the previous night's fire to bake, he added them to the meat, now beginning to sizzle.

Turning then to the last of the loaf bread left over from supper, he tore it into chunks and scattered them along the stones that encircled the pit so they could warm. A half-hour later when Gurley returned, all was ready.

"Found tracks all right," Dave said, pouring himself a cup of coffee. "Heading south. Probably lining out for the border just like you figured."

"It's about all Rufe can do. Knows he best not stay in this country. Five horses?"

Gurley settled himself on his haunches, took up his plate of food, and began to eat. "Yeh, five. Ain't nobody riding double now."

Skerrit, beginning to eat also, paused for a moment. "Even so, I doubt they're moving any faster. Horses they've got are used to pulling a wagon — or plow. They're not much good for riding."

"Don't think that'll make any difference to Rufe," Gurley said with a shrug. "All that counts with him is that they keep going. I figure we ought to be able to trim his lead plenty today — horses of ours are in fine shape after a night's rest."

Skerrit nodded, tossed the last of the food left on his plate off into the brush for the birds and small varmints that would appear as soon as they had gone.

"Ought to have Rufe and them in sight by dark," he said. "Could even catch up if we're lucky. You're still remembering our deal?"

Dave followed the warden's example and emptied his plate into the brush. "Rufe's yours — that it?"

Skerrit, his features hard-set, nodded. "That's what I mean."

"Suits me fine — just so Rufe pays for what he done to my pa, pays with his life — but I'm wondering about something, Warden."

"What's that?"

"You being a lawman — you are, ain't you?"

Skerrit, puzzled, frowned. "Deputy sheriff. Goes with the job."

"Well, ain't you sworn to bring in outlaws alive? Ain't it against your oath to kill somebody like Rufe Houston no matter how much you'd like to?"

Ben's jaw hardened. Dave Gurley had struck a nerve. He was fully aware that it was his duty to bring in Houston to be punished by the law, but he had purposely blinded himself to that trust. He felt instead a driving need to punish the man himself — not only because he was a ruthless killer, but because he had willfully destroyed a scheme that had been doing much to help many men who, by accident or from force of desperate necessity, found themselves inside the walls of the prison.

"Forget that," he said gruffly. "Houston doesn't deserve one extra minute of life. Deal stands."

"Suits me fine," Gurley said. "Just had to be sure. Anyway, I'll be there when the shooting starts. If you miss, I won't."

"I won't miss. Let's move out."

"I'm ready," Dave responded, and fell to assisting the warden in breaking camp. When the horses were saddled and loaded, he jerked a thumb at the Waring wagon. "Anything in there we ought to take? Stuff'll just go to rot."

"Can't think of anything we need," Skerrit said. "Except somebody'll come along and claim it all before too long. It's a good wagon," he added, and swung away.

Gurley pulled in beside him. He cast a final glance at the Waring horse standing off a short distance. The animal raised its head, gave them a disinterested look, and then resumed grazing. Nearby was the pile of oats and the open keg of water Dave had provided.

"I'm hoping it won't be too long before somebody comes along and claims him," he said. "Hoping, too, it won't be them wolves I heard howling last night."

Skerrit made no reply. It was now full daylight, and he had dismissed the Waring incident, the wagon, and the lone horse from his mind, having new and more important things to think about. Mostly, they must keep the trail left by Rufe Houston and his party in sight, not just assume that the outlaws were headed for the border and blindly follow.

Rufe was no fool, and whoever it was that had planned the prison break with him was equally smart. They could want to leave the impression for whoever they suspected would be following that they were hurrying to Mexico, and then turn aside, continue in a different direction. Skerrit made his thoughts known to Gurley.

Dave, riding little more than an arm's length away, eyes on the ground, nodded. "What I've been thinking, too. Rufe tried fooling us back there at Ramsey's store. Ain't nothing to say he won't try it again."

"Long as we keep his trail in front of us we'll be all right."

"Plenty plain so far," Gurley said. "Five horses leave a hell of a lot of sign. Be hard to lose track of them."

But around midmorning, with the sun out strong, Gurley suddenly pulled to a halt. Brushing his hat to the back of his head, he dismounted.

"Something happening here," he said.

Skerrit, frowning, bent forward on his saddle for a closer look at the trail. "Can see it. Looks like they've turned east. You make out if it was all of them, or just some?"

Gurley, hunched over the lightly marked prints, continued to examine them. After a bit he straightened, stared off into the east.

"All five of them," he said, returning to the buckskin. "Headed for them hills. Can't figure why."

"Neither can I," Ben Skerrit said as Gurley swung up onto his saddle. "But where they go, we go."

Both men had spurred their horses and were moving forward on the new course before Skerrit had finished speaking. They rode steadily, bearing directly into brushy, low-hill country studded with cedars, cactus, and bayonet yucca. An occasional jack-rabbit spurted out from under the horses' hooves, and once a covey of blue quail exploded from the weedy growth and soared off into the distance.

"Water up ahead," Skerrit announced, raising himself in his stirrups. "Can see some trees and rocks. Must be a spring."

"Sure didn't figure there'd be water around here," Gurley said, glancing about. "You reckon that's why Rufe and his bunch headed up this way?"

"Probably. Somebody in the group knew about the spring. Expect they camped here last night."

Gurley remained quiet, but when they drew to a halt moments later, he nodded as he came off his saddle.

"Been a fire in that pit, all right. Still smoking. And it was them."

"We best be sure," Skerrit said, maintaining his caution. "Look for tracks."

Gurley was already moving off to the side, eyes searching the damp soil around the spring's pond. Skerrit had scarcely begun his quest when Dave stopped him.

"Over here, Warden. Plenty of hoofprints and droppings. Had their horses picketed here."

Skerrit, allowing his bay to join Gurley's buckskin at the spring, crossed to where

Dave stood, noting the food scraps left by Houston's party as he did. "Next thing is to figure out for sure which way they went when they left here," he said. "They head back south or —"

"Nope," Gurley cut in, pointing to a narrow path leading into a wash a few strides farther on. The tracks of several horses lay plain in the loose, red soil. "Kept on going east."

"East," Ben echoed, his brow again drawn into deep furrows. "Rufe must feel mighty confident."

"Why? What's over that way?"

"Town called Haystack — about a half day's ride or so from here."

Dave rubbed at his stubbled jaw while a hard grin cracked his mouth. "Going to take time off for a little celebrating, I reckon. That's going to be a mistake — one that'll cost him. I've got a hunch we've caught Rufe Houston, Warden!"

"Maybe so," Skerrit agreed. "Let's get there, fast."

16

The day's heat built as they rode steadily eastward, and by noon, when they stopped to breathe the horses, it lay heavily upon the broad flat across which they were passing.

"You want a bit to eat and some coffee?" Skerrit asked as they hunkered in the meager shade of a mesquite.

Gurley shook his head. "Let it go."

Ben felt the same way. They'd had a large breakfast, and he wanted to lose no more time than necessary. They waited out a short half-hour and then mounted up and moved on. He was still puzzled as to the reason why Rufe Houston would swing off the road to Mexico, and safety, and head east.

It wouldn't be for trail supplies. According to Ramsey, the storekeeper, Rufe and his men had helped themselves liberally to his stock of merchandise. Why, then, would Rufe change his plans? True, Haystack was a wild town, running wide open with little or no law to restrict activities, and the convict need have little fear insofar as a town marshal was concerned. But by going to the settlement Rufe was putting himself farther from Mexico while at the same time placing more lawmen between himself and the security of the border.

Could the girl he'd abducted have anything to do with it? That hardly seemed possible; and ruling that out, along with the need for grub, left only the desire for whiskey — or, perhaps, a meeting with someone.

If he knew who Houston's partners were, he might be able to come up with an answer, but he'd drawn a blank at the prison when he'd made inquiries. None of the convicts had any idea who the three men who'd aided him in the break were. Nor did the guards; a big, hard-case man and two younger ones, that's all they could tell him.

Ramsey, too, was of little help, supplying the same description as the one he'd gotten at the pen. The storekeeper did recall, or thought he'd heard, one of the young ones call Houston Pa, but he couldn't be sure. He knew what Rufe was from the clothing he wore — an escaped convict — but he was unaware of the man's name until told.

If Houston had a son, the warden didn't

know it. Rufe, always closemouthed inside the walls, certainly had never mentioned it to anyone. And there were no records to say where he had come from or give any details concerning his family. It could be both of the young men were his sons, just as the older one might be a brother or other relative.

Who they were was of little consequence. Rufe had tied them in to him when he made the break; there had then been killings — several of them now — and that made them all murderers in the eyes of the law.

"You're looking mighty serious," Gurley said as they reined the horses down to a walk. "Must be hashing over something real important."

Skerrit smiled humorlessly. They were still on a vast flat, one marked only by more cholla cacti, stands of Apache plume, and occasional clumps of rabbit brush. Snakeweed were like round, green bubbles everywhere while overhead the sky was cloudless and steel blue.

"Trying to figure out why Rufe would turn east," he said.

Dave brushed at the sweat on his face. "Yeh, it's sure a puzzlement — and it don't make sense. You think he's going there for whiskey — and women?"

"Wondered about that. Could be liquor, but why women? He's got the Waring girl."

Gurley's shoulders stirred. "Well, I don't know Rufe much, but I can't see him sharing her with the others. Could be it's them wanting women and heading for Haystack to get them — along with some whiskey."

"Expect that's as good a reason as any to go on," Skerrit agreed. "Rufe's got a good opinion of himself, and he thinks he's plenty smart. Proved that back at Ramsey's when he tried to throw us off his trail — and likely thinks he did."

"About right, because he sure didn't take any pains to hide their trail once they got away from Ramsey's store. And they did at the start in that arroyo when they were on foot — before they got to his place."

Ben Skerrit shifted on his saddle, easing his back muscles. He had done but little riding in the past year or so, and that omission was making itself felt.

"Sounds like the answer," he said. "Rufe's got the idea that he's covered his trail, that nobody's following him, and it's making him careless."

"So he figures there's no harm in going

over to this town — Haystack — and all of them having themselves a big time before they go on to Mexico."

"That's the way it adds up to me," Skerrit said. "All we have to do is get there before they pull out again. Let's whip it up some."

Gurley responded by roweling his horse, and then, together, both animals broke into a lope. After a few minutes, rocking gently with the motion of his buckskin and raising his voice to be heard above the drum of hooves, he called to Skerrit. "Been thinking about that girl —"

The warden nodded. "Sure hate it."

"Bothers me aplenty."

"Don't let it," Skerrit said. "Was nothing we could do. Can see now if we'd kept going we'd probably lost their trail in the dark, when they turned east — and that would have thrown us way behind, maybe lost them for good to us. We did what we had to."

"Yeh, expect so. But it still makes me feel sort of bad," Gurley said, and glanced at the sun. Sweat again clothed his face, and there were damp spots in his shirt. "How much farther is it to that town?"

"Couple hours," Skerrit replied, slackening the pace. Looking ahead, he pointed to a line of bluffs. They were finally coming to the end of the broad plain. "Be some shade there. Can cool off a bit while we rest the horses."

Gurley made an indifferent gesture with his free hand. "No need, far as I'm concerned — and we can walk the horses for a spell. . . . You think that girl's still alive?"

"No reason to think she's not."

"Guess you're right," Dave said.

They rode on through the late-afternoon heat, alternately loping and walking their horses. They reached the bluffs, continued, and came at last to a break in the vast plain, which had appeared, for that last hour, to be moving away from them. It proved at first to be an abrupt, rock-studded lifting of the land, but on beyond the outcropping, the flat sloped gently down into a valley, green in its center with trees and grass, and brightened by the sparkle of a stream winding through it.

"Smoke!" Gurley said, pointing. "That the town down there?"

"That's it — Haystack," the warden replied, having a look back over his shoulder at the sun. "Ought to get there right about dark."

17

Despite Jace Fargo's pessimistic prediction, they reached Haystack well before dark. Halting at the edge of the town — a scattered dozen structures, most of which were devoted to liquor, gambling, and women — Rufe considered the settlement thoughtfully.

"There a lawman in this dump?" he asked.

Fargo nodded. "Sure, a marshal, but you don't have to worry none. He won't bother you — never bothers nobody."

"Then what's he here for?"

"Just for show. Knows which side of his bread the butter's on."

Rufe grunted in satisfaction. "I aim to do a mite of celebrating — make up for all the time I was in the pen. Sure don't want no two-bit tin star breathing down my neck."

"He won't be — can promise you that. Ain't hardly nothing in Haystack but saloons and bawdy houses, and the fellows that run them won't stand for the law meddling with their customers."

"Good," Rufe said, and glanced around

at Leo and Billy. "Expect you're both a-wanting to wet your whistles."

Billy half-smiled, nodded. His pa was now taking him into consideration where before such words would have been directed to Leo alone. He said, "Sure."

"Me, too," Leo said, and pointed at Jenny Waring. "What're we going to do with her? We take her into town we'll have to keep a sharp eye on her every minute, and I sure expect to be too busy doing something else for that."

Rufe rubbed at his jaw, studied the girl thoughtfully. "You're right, but I ain't ready to let her go."

"There's a old shack right over there at the end of the street," Fargo said, pointing to a small hut a hundred yards or so from the first of the structures. "Was empty last time I was here — still could be. I used it myself."

Rufe continued to scrub at the side of his broad face. "You mean I could leave her there, tied up and gagged?"

Fargo grinned. "You're wanting to hang on to her — so, why not? She'd be safe and sound and waiting for us when we got back."

"What if some drifter come along wanting to bed down in that shack? He'd find her inside," Billy pointed out, his voice a bit taut.

"Can leave the horses in the corral behind it. That'll make it look like somebody's already there."

Rufe Houston bobbed, made his decision. "That's just what I'll do," he said, and motioning to the others, rode on to the shack.

As they drew up in the corral — the gate to which was down — and dismounted, music blending with shouts and laughter was coming from the buildings along the short length of street, and down at its farther end the quick, flat crack of a pistol shot.

"Sure sounds like a right busy place," Rufe observed.

"Reckon you'll find it wide open as they come," Fargo assured the outlaw.

"Just what I'm needing," Rufe said, and beckoned to Jenny Waring. "Come on, girl."

Pointing at the shack, she shook her head stubbornly. "You ain't putting me in there!"

At Jenny's flat statement of refusal, Rufe's jaw hardened. His mouth cracked into a tight grin. "Oh, I reckon I am. Ain't taking no chance on you running off.

Figure to go have myself a few drinks, then come back. Won't be gone long."

Billy and Leo, in the act of lifting the corral gate into place, paused. Fargo, moving over to the shack, was looking inside.

"I ain't going to run away," the girl said.

"No, you sure ain't," Rufe replied, still grinning. "You ain't about to fool me. Minute we got to the first saloon you'd start bawling and yelling for somebody to help you —"

"No, I promise —"

"Place is empty," Jace Fargo called over a shoulder. "Even got a nice pile of straw there to lay on. She'll be real comfortable."

"You hear that?" Rufe asked, suddenly reaching for the girl and grasping her by the arm. "Going to be right nice —"

Jenny jerked free, started to run for the opening in the corral. Rufe lunged, again caught her, this time by the hair. She came to an abrupt halt. Her head snapped back, and Rufe, no longer smiling, slapped her hard across the face.

"Now, you listen to me, girl!" he snarled as her knees buckled. "You're doing what I say and when I say it. If I holler frog, you jump, and you better do it damn quick or you'll get more of what you just got!"

Jenny, hand to her bruised lips, drew

herself upright slowly. Hatred glowed in her eyes as she faced him.

"Damn you. Don't you ever hit me again," she said through clenched teeth.

Rufe's arm came up. His broad hand was open, ready for another blow. "You sassing me, you —"

"No, Pa!" Billy yelled, dropping his end of the gate and rushing forward. "Don't hit her again!"

Rufe, flaring anger turning him livid, spun, the blow he'd intended for the girl momentarily forgotten.

"You butting in on my business, boy? You telling me what I can't do?" he shouted, and clenching his fist, swung it at his younger son.

Billy dodged neatly, retreated a few steps. "I am, Pa. It ain't right you knocking her around like that."

Jenny had lowered her hand, was staring at Rufe coldly. "He ain't hurt me none," she said. "I'm plenty used to beatings from my pa. Him and Grandpa there are just alike. Ain't happy unless they're slapping somebody littler than them around.

"I'm telling you now, Grandpa, I ain't all that weak! Now, maybe you figure you've snared yourself a little turtledove, but you sure'n hell ain't! The next time you hit me,

I'll kill you. Not sure how, but I'll kill you!"

Rufe Houston's eyes spread. His thick brows lifted, and he laughed, stepped forward. Before Jenny could move he seized her by an arm, yanked her about. Then, drawing back his open palm, he slapped her again. The girl moaned, went limp onto the ground.

"Damn it, Pa!" Billy yelled, and hurried toward her.

Rufe's big hand went. Long fingers caught his younger son by the neck and, swinging him around, threw him hard against the wall of the shack.

"Can see I'm going to have to learn you some manners," Rufe said, watching Billy pull himself back onto his feet. "You got yourself some bad habits while I was away, but it'll have to wait. Some other things I'm needing to do right now."

Bending down, the outlaw picked up the half-conscious girl as easily as if she were a small child, and jerking his head at Fargo, started for the door of the shack.

"Bring that there rawhide cord I seen you fiddling with, Jace, and help me tie up this here little wildcat of mine. Can use your bandanna, too. Got to keep her from yelling."

Fargo, unwinding a narrow length of leather from around his waist, fell in behind Rufe as he carried Jenny into the hut and laid her on the pile of straw. Handing the rawhide to Houston, he removed the bandanna from around his neck and, fashioning a gag, tied it over the girl's mouth.

"You be dang sure that's tight," Rufe warned. "I don't want her yelling and somebody coming in and turning her loose. Sure would be disappointed was me to come back after a bit and find her gone."

Fargo nodded. "She'll be all right. Had to leave it a little slack so's she can breathe."

Rufe, finished with binding Jenny's hands behind her back, was now engaged in firmly linking her ankles together.

"She's a perky little rascal, ain't she," he said, more as a statement of fact than a question. "You see her stand right up there and sass me? I like that."

Fargo had drawn himself upright, was leaning against the side of the hut. "You sure got yourself a right funny way of showing it — hitting her like you did. She's going to be laid out for quite a spell — a hour at least."

"Man has to treat a woman that way —

let her know who's the boss. And they like it."

"I ain't so sure about her liking it," Fargo said with a half-smile. "Was I you, Rufe, I'd be mighty damn careful about turning my back on her if there was a knife or a gun handy."

Rufe laughed. "You just don't know women! Come morning, that little gal will be eating out of my hand. . . . Come on, let's hightail it to the first saloon —"

"Best one's called the Sidewinder. Lot of fancy women there — and gambling and dancing, too, if you're of a mind."

"The Sidewinder, then. I'm mighty anxious to get started on some serious drinking."

"And womaning —"

"Nope, I got one right here. Like I said, soon's I swallow me a few drinks, I'm coming back to her."

"Gates all set, Pa," Leo called from the doorway. "Reckon we're ready."

"So're we," Rufe answered, and motioning Fargo by, followed him into the open and pulled the sagging door of the shack closed.

18

Jenny Waring opened her eyes. It was full dark, but she knew immediately where she was and what had happened. Rufe had hit her, knocked her senseless, and then he or one of the others had carried her into the shack and laid her on a pile of straw.

Her head was aching dully and she was finding it a bit hard to breathe. Whoever had put the gag over her mouth and nose had done a good job of it. The same applied to the cords that bound her wrists and ankles. They had been drawn so tightly that they cut into her flesh and were hindering circulation.

She stirred, endeavored to sit up, finally managed it by squaring herself about until her shoulders were against the wall. It didn't help her breathing or lessen the pain in her hands or legs any, but it was somewhat more comfortable. She guessed she could stand the pain until Rufe returned; it was no stranger to her.

There was no way to see beyond the walls of the old shack, although starlight was seeping through the cracks between the boards and the one uncovered window. Music, too, was reaching her by the same route, coming from the saloons in the settlement. It was good, lively music, and Jenny found herself wishing she were there enjoying it.

She had no idea how long Rufe would be gone; for a couple of hours, at least. The others likely wouldn't return until morning. Maybe, if she listened carefully and watched her chances, someone might pass close enough to the shack to hear her and set her free. She could kick on the wall, set up a noise that way.

But Jenny Waring wasn't certain that was what she really wanted. It was actually thrilling to be mixed up with a gang of outlaws, and that's just what she'd been looking for all her life — thrills and excitement.

She wasn't exactly too thrilled, however, at being claimed by old Rufe Houston, the escaped convict. He was like her pa, downright mean, and she'd had more than enough slapping around to suit her.

But Rufe had claimed her, and none of the others had sand enough to buck him. Billy, his younger son, had shown a bit of spunk a couple of times, and earlier she had decided, more or less, to cozy up to him. It might — and it might not — be the thing to do; she'd best let matters ride awhile longer before she made up her mind.

Actually Rufe was the head of the bunch, and being in close with the boss-man was the logical way to go. But Rufe was not only a little old for her, but like her pa, was also too handy with his fists.

The other man — Jace, they called him — was some years younger. He'd barely noticed her, however, treated her almost as if she didn't exist. She reckoned it was that peculiar sort of honor observed by the majority of men; she was Rufe's woman and a hands-off policy was strictly observed.

Rufe's son Leo evidently didn't subscribe to that principle, although he was most careful to see that his pa was unaware of it. Several times she'd caught him looking her over with a sort of gleam in his eyes — like the boys and the men who came by the homestead or she encountered in town always did.

And there was that time — the previous evening, in fact — while Rufe was sleeping off the whiskey he'd drunk, that Leo had tried to get her off to one side and Billy had stopped him. Billy's show of fight had surprised his brother, just as it had her.

Jenny shifted about, attempting to relieve her cramped muscles. The music from the saloons had become louder, and she guessed things were in full swing throughout the settlement.

She liked Billy, and while he had shown no particular interest in her, except of sympathy, she had a feeling that he would if it wasn't for his pa — and that could be changing. Billy was different from what he had been when she'd first met him. He was beginning to defy the old man at times and no longer just stood and took the abuse Rufe handed out.

Billy, Jenny decided all at once, was the one for her — the one she'd line up with and stick to in the days to come. She wasn't too sure in her mind just how she'd handle Rufe, but she'd manage somehow. Earlier she'd told him flat out she'd kill him if he hit her again, and he'd just laughed and gone right ahead and knocked her cold.

She had been mad as hell at him at the time, and she still meant what she'd said, but whether Rufe actually believed her or she'd ever get the chance to go through with the threat was a question. One thing for sure, she'd meant it, and if Rufe realized that, maybe he'd be a bit cautious around her. Regardless, she'd somehow manage. Despite being young, she'd always had the knack of handling boys and men, with the exception of her pa, so she guessed she'd be able to come up with a scheme for taking care of Rufe and making Billy her man without too much trouble.

They could have a fine time together on their own. She would work right with Billy, help him plan out the robberies or holdups, and be his partner in every sense of the word. She could learn to use a pistol — she was fair with a shotgun, having done a bit of rabbit and quail hunting around the farm — but she didn't like shooting the long-barrel weapon, for the recoil invariably knocked her off balance and left her shoulder sore.

But a pistol was something else, and given a little time and instruction, she could become as good as any man. As for riding a horse, she'd never spent much time astride, had usually done her traveling in the family wagon or someone's buckboard. That, too, was something that could be learned. A horse was a horse no matter if you rode on him or behind him.

The job that faced her, if she was to realize her dreams, was to build up Billy, keep him going on the course he'd already begun to follow. That meant encouraging him when he took it upon himself to stand up to the others — as he did Leo that morning and his pa that afternoon. And she must remember to back him when he proposed an idea or suggested a plan or offered an opinion.

And when it came to facing up to Rufe, let Billy know that she believed he was doing the right thing regardless of what it was all about. She must create a feeling of independence in him, and then, when the right opportunity presented itself, she'd convince him that they would be better off on their own and that they should pull out, leave Rufe and the others flat.

They were headed for Mexico, something about a deal with a friend of Jace Fargo's that would get them a lot of gold. Like as not Billy wouldn't want to miss out on that, and Jenny guessed it would be smart to wait until he got his share and then strike out on their own. One thing, if Rufe had his way, Billy would come in for a very small share. It would be up to her to see that Billy got what was coming to him. If they . . .

Jenny Waring's thoughts came to a halt. The doorway of the shack had opened and a dark figure stood silhouetted against the night. If it was Rufe . . .

"Howdy —"

A slight flow of relief passed through the girl. It was Leo, voice recognizable despite a distinct thickening from liquor. Of the two men, he was the lesser to be contended with; she hadn't as yet figured out how to cope with Rufe.

"Come to pay you a little visit — Pa and the others being real busy right about now."

Jenny struggled against her bonds, tried to speak through the gag that was crushing her lips. All that came out were muffled sounds.

"Now, don't you worry none about Pa," Leo said, entering the hut and pulling the door closed. "He's having hisself a big time with a little redhead. Others've got themselves a gal, too.

"But me, I kept thinking about you back here in the dark all by yourself and feeling lonesome and wanting some company —"

Jenny again shifted about, straining at the cords that bound her wrists and ankles while she tried to speak, to warn him of the consequences of his act if he went through with what he had in mind. Leo seemed to know what she was thinking.

"Done told you — don't fret none about

Pa finding out about us. I sure ain't going to tell him, and you ain't either because I'll kill you if you do. I'll just watch my chances and put a knife into you, or maybe there'll be a shooting — accidental —"

Leo, crouching before her, paused. Turning his head, he listened. Jenny, too, had heard the sound — the soft thud of horses approaching the shack. The noise stopped, somewhere near the corral. A voice, barely audible, reached her and Leo.

"It's them, all right. Five horses — all farm stock. Left them here while they went into town."

A different voice said, "Expect we'll find them in one of the saloons —"

"Just where they'll be — and there's a half a dozen or more of them. Best we get at it. I don't want them slipping through my fingers."

The muted beat of hooves resumed, faded shortly. Leo got to his feet quickly, turned for the door.

"Got to warn Pa," he said, and slipping through the doorway, hurried off into the night.

19

"Best we take it slow," Ben Skerrit said as they drew near the town. It was night and Haystack was a noisy strip of pale-yellow light in the darkness.

"Sure are whooping it up down there," Gurley remarked, cocking his head to one side that he might better hear the music.

"It's that kind of a town," Skerrit explained. "Fit only for outlaws on the run, trail drivers blowing their wages, and drifters. Won't find much else around."

"No lawman?"

"There's a marshal — so he calls himself. Looks after the drunks."

They had come to the end of the street. Skerrit drew to a halt. "Hard telling which saloon Rufe and his bunch will be in," he said, considering the row of structures.

Some were lighted outside, had painted signs, and there was one with a high false front that rose above all else. Most, however, were plain, one-story buildings that had no illumination other than the faint glow that spilled through an open door or window to indicate it was open for business.

There were three or four places in total darkness. They would be the nonsaloons that existed in the town, a gunsmith, saddlery, general store, and the like. A fair number of horses stood, weary, dim shadows in the murk, at the hitchracks along the dusty way, and such led to the belief that somewhere a cattle drive had been concluded and the crew en route back to the ranch were celebrating.

"How you figure to do that?" Gurley asked, pulling his pistol and, with the aid of the moonlight, checking to see that all ports in the cylinder were full.

"The Sidewinder Saloon — over there," the warden replied, pointing at the building that appeared to be enjoying the major share of activity. "It's the biggest, and I reckon you could say the best. Always a lot going on in there, and there're plenty of women hanging around. I've got a hunch that's where we'll find Rufe. It's been a long time for him between drinks and women."

"That girl, the homesteader's daughter —"

"Probably with them. Rufe's not the kind to let her hold him back."

The doorway of the saloon first in the

row along the street suddenly filled and then several men burst into the open. Two were locked in each other's arms, were wrestling from side to side, while a half a dozen onlooking friends shouted advice and encouragement.

Suddenly the battlers broke apart, steadied themselves, and began to trade blows. One went to his knees. Cheers arose and the small crowd closed in on the fighters. Shortly all wheeled and reentered the saloon.

When all had returned to normalcy, Gurley said, "Rufe's the only one I know on sight. Going to be a bit hard picking them out of a bunch like we just seen — if he's off somewhere — unless you've got some names and descriptions."

"Same goes for me — Rufe's the only one I could spot. Did get a bit of a rundown from the guards and the convicts. And you heard Ramsey say that he thought one of the boys called Houston Pa."

"He wasn't dead sure —"

"No, and I guess we can't bank on it, but if it's true, it could be he'll look like Rufe and that'll tip us off. And there's the older man, about Rufe's age. He's redheaded. That'll help."

Gurley spun the cylinder of his pistol

thoughtfully, thrust the weapon back into its holster. "Expect the only for-certain thing is to find Rufe hisself —"

"About the size of it," the warden agreed, roweling his horse lightly. "Let's have a look first off at the Sidewinder's customers."

They rode on into the street, keeping to its east side beyond the flare of lamplight in the event the outlaws should be looking. Reaching the Sidewinder, they halted at its rack, dismounted, and tied their horses alongside several others already there.

"Watch my back," Skerrit said, and crossing the landing to the door, stepped into the swirl of noise, smoke, and smells.

Pausing just within the brightly lit room, he glanced about, meeting head-on the narrow looks of several patrons who observed his entrance and that of Dave Gurley, standing close on his heels, hand resting on the butt of his pistol. There was no sign of Houston and his partners, but they could be in one of the back rooms.

Aware of the silence that had fallen and ignoring the curious, even resentful stares at him — he was being taken for a lawman, he knew — Skerrit cut his way across the floor toward the bar that ran almost the width of the rear wall. Reaching it, he halted, let his cool gaze again sweep the room, and then put his attention on the lone bartender.

"Looking for Rufe Houston," he stated. "He'd have three others with him — redhead about his age and two younger. Could be his sons. Likely was a girl with them."

The bartender shrugged indifferently. "Ain't seen none of them."

Skerrit's jaw hardened. Something in the man's eyes, or perhaps it was his manner, said he was lying. "Give it some more thought. You came up with that a mite fast."

"Don't take long to think," the bartender replied. "Ain't seen no Rufe or nobody that was with him."

The warden continued to study the man coldly. "He in the back — that it? Or maybe out in one of the shacks with some women?"

The bartender shook his head stubbornly. "Said he wasn't around —"

"Then you won't be caring if me and my partner goes back and looks around —"

"Damn it! You heard what Arnie said!" a voice down the bar cut in suddenly. "Don't you savvy English?"

Gurley, standing beyond Skerrit, pulled

away from the counter a step and faced the speaker, a squat cowhand, pretty much in his cups, wearing a scarred leather vest over a new checked shirt and other trail clothing.

"Keep your nose in your own glass of beer, mister," Dave warned softly. "My friend's talking to the barkeep, not you."

"He ain't listening good, else he's too dumb to —"

"Maybe he figures Arnie ain't telling him the truth."

"Well, maybe he'll believe this!" the cowhand shouted, and fists doubled, lunged at Skerrit.

Ben jerked aside as the blow skimmed past his head. In the next instant his knuckled hand shot out, caught the cowhand on the point of the jaw, and sent him to his knees. Instantly yells went up, followed by a scuffing of boot heels as the cowhand's friends started to close in. The sharp crack of Gurley's pistol brought them to a halt.

"Back off," he ordered, drifting the smoking muzzle of his pistol back and forth over the crowd, facing him and Skerrit in an irregular line. "Back off — or the next bullet won't be going into the roof."

The warden had drawn his pistol also, was narrowly watching the man he had floored, alert for any sign of further trouble, but the cowhand, drawing himself painfully to his feet, showed no inclination to continue the incident. Holding a hand to his jaw, he glared at Skerrit.

"Sure would like to meet up with you again somewheres. I just ain't feeling too good right now," he mumbled.

Skerrit's hard mouth cracked into a tight smile. "Doubt that'll ever happen, but I'll be proud to accommodate you if it ever does."

"You a lawman?"

Skerrit shook his head. "You see a badge?"

The cowhand shrugged. "Nope, but that don't mean you ain't got one tucked inside your pocket. Them that comes here usually does it that way. Ain't got the guts to wear their star where a fellow can see it."

The crowd halted by Gurley had begun to drift away, return to whatever had been occupying their attention now that the excitement was over.

"Don't know about that, but I'm no regular lawman. Was once — I'll give you that much. Was a few years ago."

"Then why're you so all fired set on

finding this jasper — Rufe? You got something to settle with him — a beef maybe?"

"Can call it that," the warden said, and turned again to Arnie the bartender. "How about it? You ready to answer my questions, or are me and my friend going to start a free-for-all in your place?"

Arnie glanced around, swallowed hard. The cowhand, leaning slackly against the bar, nodded.

"Whyn't you go ahead and tell him? He ain't no badge-toter, and I sure didn't cotton to that Rufe, anyway. Was a wise son of a bitch — knowed everything there was to know, to hear him tell it."

Arnie laid the towel he was holding to one side, smiled thinly. "Him shining up to your gal, Ruby, wouldn't have nothing to do with that, would it, Charlie?"

The cowhand swore, moved back to his original place at the counter, and took up his drink. Arnie, a bottle now in his hand, looked questioningly at Skerrit, who nodded. The barman produced two clean glasses, filled them, shoved them forward to Gurley and the warden, and then waited pointedly for his pay. That taken care of, he nodded.

"They was here — Rufe and his two boys and a redheaded jasper he called Jace."

"No girl?" Gurley asked, frowning.

"Nope, sure didn't bring one in here. They left just before you come in. One of the boys went outside for something, then pretty soon come running back. Talked to Rufe and them — they was all back here at that corner table with a couple of the gals — then they just up all of a sudden and took off out the back door."

Ben Skerrit swore deeply, angrily. Houston had been within his reach, but had slipped through his fingers. Someone — apparently one of Rufe's sons — had spotted Gurley and him, had warned the outlaw.

Skerrit shrugged wearily, downed his whiskey, and pointed at the empty glass. "Fill it up again, and have one yourself."

He should have had no kind feeling toward the bartender, who, by refusing to answer questions, had given the outlaws more time to escape. But there was nothing to be gained in deploring the fact; what was done, was done. Rufe, with his two sons and a friend called Jace, had gotten away — and there was nothing to do but start over.

"What do you reckon happened to the girl?" he heard Gurley say.

Raising his glass, Ben swallowed his

whiskey in a single gulp. "Wouldn't know."

Dave studied the tall man for a long minute. Then, "You aiming to ride on after them tonight? Mite dark out there and finding — and keeping — a trail'll be hard."

"We'll wait for first light," Skerrit replied, turning and leaning against the bar. "Can start then."

20

Skerrit and Gurley had spent the remainder of the night in the Sidewinder, having a meal in that part of the saloon set aside for those who wanted food and getting a few hours' sleep in one of the back rooms. The horses, too, had benefitted from the enforced delay, Gurley having located a livery barn, run by a blacksmith, at the end of the street where he stabled the animals and saw to their care and feeding.

Now, with the day's first flare of light spreading across the land to fade the shadows of night, they drew up at the old corral at the edge of the settlement where they had seen the outlaws' horses. Lounging idly on his saddle while Dave searched about for tracks that would indicate the direction that Rufe and his party had taken, Skerrit gave the nearby shack thought.

The girl — Jenny — had not been with them when they went to the Sidewinder that previous night, but there had been five horses waiting in the corral. He doubted

Rufe would bother with an extra mount — he'd not taken the one that remained of Noah Waring's team — therefore, it was logical to think that the girl was still alive and with him.

On a hunch Ben rode up to the hut and, staying on the bay, pushed open the door. It was still half-dark inside the small structure, but he immediately saw a pile of straw in one corner that appeared to have been recently stirred about. Nearby were the remnants of some rawhide cord.

"Come across something?" Gurley asked, halting beside the bay. He had turned from his search for hoofprints, was leading his buckskin.

"Looks like the girl was probably in here last night," Skerrit said. "Rufe was scared to take her into town, figured she might set up a holler. So they tied her up with rawhide and left her here."

Gurley swung up onto his saddle, settled himself, spat in disgust. "And we wasn't no more'n two jumps away when we was looking at them horses."

"Can bet Rufe had her gagged so's she couldn't make a sound. . . . Which way did they head out?"

"South. Looks like they're pointing for Mexico again."

"Then we best be moving," Skerrit said, cutting the bay about and pulling away. "They've got a good start on us, and Rufe knows now that we're on his trail."

Gurley nodded. "He'll ride hard, but there's still a couple of things in our favor. Horses they're forking ain't fast, and they ain't had much rest."

"I'm counting on that," Skerrit said, looking ahead to the land that rolled out to all directions in a pale-green-and-tan carpet marred only here and there by clumps of brush. "Glad to know the girl's still alive."

Dave Gurley, swaying gently with the motion of his loping horse, shook his head. "Ain't sure her being alive in the hands of Rufe Houston and his bunch is better than being dead."

"Can't talk for women," Skerrit said, "but it's been my experience that staying alive beats everything."

They rode on under the now-climbing sun. The country changed from broad prairie to low, rolling hills covered with grass, and back again. Mountains began to loom against the horizon in the east, ragged, smoky blue-gray formations that tore the cloud-free sky. The heat mounted, became oppressive, and near noon, when they dropped down into a narrow valley, the center of which was marked by a small cluster of cottonwood trees, Skerrit pointed out the oasislike area to Gurley.

"Be a good place to rest the horses. Likely a spring there."

"Suits me," Dave called back. "Can use a cup of coffee, maybe even a bite to eat."

The coffee sounded good to Ben Skerrit, but he was not hungry. They had enjoyed a large breakfast of eggs, steak, and all the trimmings at the Sidewinder before leaving that morning — a meal that would hold him until dark.

"Horses there," Gurley said, again raising his voice to be heard. "Can see a couple."

Skerrit had caught sight of the animals, too. They were standing, heads low, at the edge of the grove. Whoever was riding them was not visible.

"Swing wide," the warden said, caution dictating their approach. "Don't think it's any of Rufe's bunch, but we best be sure before we ride in."

At once Gurley cut away to his left while Ben Skerrit veered to the opposite direction, but as they drew nearer, neither could locate the riders of the two mounts. And then Skerrit, coming in from behind a clump of willows growing along the spring-fed pond, pulled up.

Two men lay on the ground a short distance from the horses. Both appeared to be dead. Signaling to Dave, the warden drew his pistol and moved in slowly.

There was no need for care. One of the two was dead; the other, badly wounded, had but a few minutes of life remaining. Gurley, pausing, had picked up a dented cup when he recognized the situation, had filled it with water from the spring, and was hurrying with it to ease the dying man's thirst. Evidently the two — cowhands, from their outfits — had stopped in the coolness of the grove to make coffee, and had been bushwhacked.

"Sure — glad you — come along," the man mumbled feebly, gulping down the water. "Name's — name's Gilmore. Hated dying — here. Coyotes — buzzards'd come — and —"

"What happened?" Skerrit asked. "Who shot you?"

"Big fellow. Was — four of them — and a girl —"

"Rufe," Skerrit said in a low, raspy voice.

He was holding the cup again to Gilmore's ups, but anger was throbbing through him so intensely that his hand trembled. Two more killings to Houston's credit! Two more murders that he, personally, was responsible for!

"They — rode in — real friendly-like," Gilmore continued. And then, as if realizing what Skerrit had said, added, "You — know them? They — friends — of your'n?"

"Not by a damn sight!" Skerrit snapped. "They're outlaws — killers. We've been trailing them. Why'd they shoot you?"

Gurley said, "Look at them horses, Warden. You'll get your answer there."

Ben shifted his glance to the animals. Both were heavy-bodied farm stock and wore only bridles.

"Was — our horses they — wanted," Gilmore said. "Big fellow says — you — want to do some — horse trading? I said — nope. Then — he just — ups and draws — his iron — and lets go at me and — and Amos. Killed Amos right off. Left — me here — for — the coyotes —"

Skerrit settled back on his heels, features cold, eyes partly closed. Rufe had now killed four persons in cold blood since he'd broken out — not counting the convicts who had apparently wanted to accompany him or the guard or guards who had attempted to stop him.

But Rufe was a dead man. He'd find the outlaw, get him, kill him if it took the rest of his own life. Rufe would never get away — never!

"Took our irons — too," Gilmore muttered. "Was we — knowing — they wanted them horses — that bad — Amos and me'd a' just handed — them over. Sure — was no — call to go and — shoot us for — a couple — of damn — broomtails."

Gilmore's voice had weakened and his words were slurred. He let his eyes close slowly, and then abruptly opened them and clutched at the warden's arm.

"You — you won't — be leaving — me and Amos just a-laying — here — will you, mister? You'll — bury us — so's the coyotes and —"

"We'll take care of you and your partner," Ben reassured him. "Don't fret about it. Just lay back and take it easy."

Gilmore's eyes closed again. A faint smile plucked at the corners of his mouth. "Sure — obliged," he murmured, and went slack.

They buried the two men in a dry wash not far from the spring, placing them well back where spring-rain runoff couldn't reach them, and then caving in the banks so that they would be completely covered over. After that they removed the bridles from the two horses — once the property of Noah Waring or Ramsey — and set them free that they could graze unhampered.

When that was done, Skerrit, grim-faced and determined, swung back onto his saddle. Gurley, equally affected by Rufe Houston's callousness, mounted also, and together they resumed the outlaws' trail.

21

Rufe Houston swore savagely. How the hell did those tin stars get on his trail so damn fast? And who were they?

He'd been dead certain he'd left no tracks back at that arroyo and at the general store where they'd stopped that anybody could pick up — yet here was a lousy pair of badge-toters right on his heels! In fact, if Leo hadn't spotted them there at the shack, they likely would have run smack-dab into them at the saloon.

Rufe scrubbed irritably at the back of his neck as they loped steadily southward. Leo's seeing the two lawmen when and where he did . . . but now that he had time to think about it, just what the hell was Leo doing there? It hadn't occurred to him earlier — being in a hell of a hurry to get out of town — but now that it came to mind, Rufe decided the boy needed to do a bit of explaining. If he was there, fooling around the little gal . . .

Jaw set angrily, Rufe looked ahead. They were traveling fairly fast since they'd run across those two cowpokes and gotten themselves a pair of better horses. He and Jace had taken them, given their mounts to Billy and the girl. Now everybody had a saddle, which was accounting, chiefly, for the better time they were making.

That was good. With the law on their tails they needed to reach the border as fast as possible — and their chances were better now. But if those two lawmen, whoever they were, managed somehow to cut down their lead, get too close, then he and Jace would make a run for it. On the cow ponies they'd have a chance.

"They ain't taking me in again," he said, wiping away the sweat on his whiskered face.

"What's that?" Fargo asked from nearby. It was near midafternoon and the heat was pitiless. "You say something?"

"Was talking to myself, I reckon," Rufe replied. "Thinking about them badge-toters. Was telling myself I wasn't letting them bastards take me back to hang. They'll have to kill me."

"Goes for me, too," Fargo said, nodding. "They'll be wanting to string me up, too, now. I don't aim to let them do it. What about your boys? They feel the same way?"

"Expect so. But ain't neither one of them

ever done any time in the pen — only in the county jail or maybe a few days in some hick-town hoosegow, so they ain't never had a real taste of being locked up."

"They ain't looking at being locked up," Jace said, swabbing his neck with his bandanna. "They're looking at a rope, same as us. You think they'll be willing to shoot it out with them lawmen if it comes down to it?"

Rufe gave that thought. "Couple of days ago I would've said yes. Both of them would've done what I told them to and no back talk. Ain't so sure now — especially of Billy."

Jace nodded, continued to mop at his face and neck. The heat had become so intense that it not only dried the lips and mouth but also was causing the eyes to smart.

"Seen that. That boy's sure changed. He don't back off at all in saying what he pleases. Seems to me us grabbing that girl and bringing her along's what done it. Sort of put some starch in his backbone."

Rufe said nothing, but the identical thought had occurred to him. Well, that was another verse to the song that was going to get sung as soon as they pulled up to spell off the horses. He had a couple of things to say to both of the boys — and that waggle-tail girl, too.

Twisting about, Rufe threw a glance to their back trail. There was no sign of riders, not even a distant dust cloud that would indicate horses on the move. He had a good lead on the lawmen, he reckoned, several hours at least. It could even be longer, all depending on how soon they'd been able to pick up tracks at the old corral.

And they hadn't stopped since encountering those two cowpokes and taking their horses. Rufe guessed a halt was due, and that it would be safe. Raising an arm, he pointed to a low bluff a quarter-mile off the trail. A shadow lying along its base offered a bit of shade.

"Pull over there," he directed, and not waiting for any reaction on the part of the others, immediately swung his horse toward the formation. Arriving there first, he drew up, came off his saddle, and uncorking his canteen, had himself a swallow of the tepid water.

The remainder of the party, filing in behind him, followed suit — except for Jenny Waring. She continued to sit her horse for several moments, and then, coming stiffly off its back, she crossed to the narrow band of shade, sighed wearily, and sat down.

"You figure it's smart to haul up here, Pa?" Leo asked. His clothing showed dark patches where sweat had soaked through and his skin had an oily shine. "Them law-dogs are bound to be coming on pretty fast."

Rufe corked his canteen and, with slow, deliberate movements, returned it to its place on his saddle. "Yeh, reckon they are," he said, "but we best blow these horses. And while we're waiting, I want to know what you was doing there at that old shack last night when you spotted them. We was all in the saloon — leastwise, that's what I was thinking."

Leo pulled off his hat, ran fingers through his damp hair. From close by, Billy watched with narrowed eyes while Jenny stared off across the flats to the west, shimmering with heat.

"I just sort of got to worrying about her, Pa," Leo said, "so I took me a walk back there to see if she was all right. You sure done a good job tying her up tight."

"He's lying, Pa," Billy said calmly. "He went there because he was wanting her. I had to make him leave her alone the other night."

Leo turned to his brother, stared at him coldly. "He's the one that's lying, Pa. He's after the girl hisself. If you don't believe me, ask her. She'll tell you that I ain't bothered her and that I truly went to that old shack to see if she was all right. Just you ask her."

Rufe walked slowly to where Jenny was sitting with folded arms. He looked down at her. "That right, girl? Did Leo come there just to see if you was all right?"

Jenny remained silent, continued to gaze off into the distance. Impatient, Rufe bent down, seized her by an arm, and shook her roughly.

"You hear me? You best answer me, girl!"

She shifted her attention to him. Her eyes were swollen slightly and partly closed, and her lips, cracked and blistered from the sun and wind, were a tight line. After a bit she nodded.

"What about that Billy was telling — about him making Leo leave you be? That true?"

Jenny hesitated briefly, said, "No."

Billy shrugged. "She's lying, because she's scared. He probably told her he'd kill her if she —"

Rufe heard Leo mutter a curse, felt the

brush of his arm as he lunged at Billy. The younger son, taken unexpectedly, staggered back as Leo crashed into him, and then, recovering quickly, caught Leo about the waist. Locked together, they began to wrestle back and forth.

Rufe, stepping back away from their heaving bodies, glanced at Fargo, grinned. "Seen this a-coming. Ain't nothing to do but let them fight it out. Surprises me some again. Billy ain't never been one to cross his brother."

Fargo's shoulders stirred. "Reckon he didn't have no choosings. Leo jumped him."

"After Billy'd called him a liar and tried to get him in trouble with me."

"Well, he's sure holding his own with Leo. Won't surprise me none if he comes out on top."

"Ain't likely," Rufe said confidently.

In that moment the combatants, wheezing and puffing for breath, broke apart, paused. Suddenly Leo rushed forward. As Billy crouched to meet the charge, the older boy bent swiftly, caught up a handful of sand, and threw it into his brother's face.

Billy cursed, fell back a step, spitting and rubbing at his eyes. Leo, fists knotted, bore in close and swung hard. The blow struck Billy on the ear, dropped him as if he'd been poleaxed.

Rufe grinned at Jace Fargo. "Can see Leo ain't forgot none of the tricks I taught him about fighting. Man wins any way he can."

Leo had stepped back, was rubbing the knuckles of his right hand. Billy, flat on the ground, was beginning to move, while Jenny, from her place at the foot of the bluff, had turned, was staring at him thoughtfully. It was as if she had considered him her champion, but now defeated, was having second thoughts. Or perhaps she was ruing a miscalculation.

"Come on, boy, get up!" Rufe said, crossing to where Billy lay. "You ain't all that bad hurt."

Billy rolled over, pulled himself to hands and knees. He hung there briefly, shook his head as if to clear it, and then drew himself upright. Dirt and bits of leaves and twigs were plastered to his sweat-covered skin as he unsteadily faced Rufe.

"You recollect me saying back a ways — at that old corral when you stuck your nose in where it didn't belong — that I'd take care of you later?" Rufe demanded.

Billy nodded woodenly, still not fully recovered.

"And now you go lying to me, boy," the outlaw continued. "That's something I sure don't put up with — and you damn well know it!"

Abruptly Rufe swung his arm. His balled fist connected with Billy's jaw, dropping him to the ground once more.

Leo laughed, nodded admiringly at Rufe. "Pa, being locked up in the pen like you was sure didn't hurt you none. You still got a wallop like a mule kicking!"

Houston considered his older son dispassionately. "Best you don't forget that," he warned, and shifted his attention to Jenny. "Get one of them canteens of water, girl, and wake Billy up. We best get to riding."

Jenny, riding alongside Billy, looked at him closely. Beyond him Jace, Rufe, and Leo, in that order, were carrying on a conversation about something that had taken place back in the saloon at Haystack. The horses were down to a slow walk in the driving heat, Rufe electing to grant them rest in that manner rather than halting entirely.

"You hurt much?" she asked, voice only high enough for him to hear.

He had taken two blows to the head and had been prepared for neither. Thus both had rocked him terribly.

"I'm all right," he replied grudgingly. "And it ain't over yet — far as I'm concerned."

"Meaning?"

"I should've known Leo'd trick me somehow, but it won't happen the next time. Next time I'll kill him."

Spirits lifting, Jenny smiled. Maybe she hadn't made a bad choice after all! Billy just needed encouragement and help to build his confidence.

"Why'd you lie when Pa asked you about Leo? You scared of him?"

She had been expecting the question. "I guess I am," she replied haltingly. "Said he'd kill me if I ever told on him, and I wasn't sure about you — about you looking out for me."

"That what you'd like for me to do?"

"It is, Billy — in the worst way. And I knew after you got to fighting Leo that it was for me. I'm obliged and thankful to you."

"Well, he was lying —"

"You bet he was! It was just the way you said. And it'd been different if them lawmen hadn't come along in time. What about your pa? You going to call his hand, too?"

Billy gave that thought, swiped at the

sweat on his face with a forearm. "Can tell you this — I ain't taking no more slapping around from him! Made up my mind to that."

Jenny smiled, reached out, and laid her hand on his arm. "That's what I was hoping to hear you say. I know now for certain that I want to be your woman — not your pa's or Leo's or anybody else's — just yours."

Billy turned a puzzled face to her. "I ain't sure I —"

"We can do some talking tonight, if I can keep your pa away. I've got big plans for me and you — for us."

"Us?" Billy echoed in wonderment.

Jenny nodded. "Soon as we get your share of that Mexican gold, we're pulling out — you and me — on our own. There's a fine, big life out there waiting for us, Billy, and we're going to grab on to it."

22

"It's smoke," Jace Fargo said, shading his eyes with a cupped hand. "I don't recollect there being no town around here."

They had just topped out a low rise and halted to breathe the horses. The day's heat had not lessened but was continuing to hammer at them, man and beast alike, with relentless fury despite the waning afternoon.

"It's something," Billy said, "can see that plain. Could be a ranch, or maybe a homesteader."

"I'd kind of like that," Rufe said, licking his dry lips. "Getting on toward supper-time and I could use a right good meal. Ain't nothing about the little gal's cooking that's good — can sure say that," he added, and winked broadly at Jenny. "I'm hoping she's a lot better at something else!"

Leo laughed and Fargo joined in. Billy, features set, one side of his face now discolored and swollen, appeared not to hear. As for Jenny Waring, she kept her eyes straight ahead and ignored the outlaw's words.

"You figure she is, Billy?" Rufe continued. His eyes had narrowed, and he was no longer in a humorous mood.

The youngest Houston shrugged indifferently. "I wouldn't be knowing."

"It's a good thing you don't," Rufe snapped, and grinned at Jenny. "Aim to get around to you sooner or later, girl — maybe tonight. It's just that something keeps coming up. Don't you fret about it."

"I ain't," Jenny said flatly.

Rufe studied her for a time and then brought back onto the thin, dirty gray wisp of smoke twisting up into the sky to the south.

"I reckon that'll be coming from some hayshaker's place," he said. "This sure ain't cattle country. Let's get along."

They rode on, the sun driving at them from the side. For a while the tracer etched against the clear blue above seemed to get no nearer, simply hung there above the horizon, neither fading nor getting more definite. And then finally, when there was little more than an hour remaining before sunset, they came to the rim of a broad swale and saw a closely grouped collection of small structures, a few trees, several well-tended fields green with produce lying in its center. The bright sparkle of water denoted the presence of a spring.

"Now, ain't that a pretty sight?" Rufe said. "I'm sure going to enjoy my vittles tonight!"

Fargo placed a hand on the horn of his saddle, raised himself in the stirrups, and looked back to the north. "You figure we can chance stopping, Rufe? Them lawmen can't be —"

"There ain't no sign of them, is there?" the outlaw demanded. "And there ain't been! Damn it. I'm getting mighty tired of somebody asking me something like that every time I want to pull up! We got plenty of time."

"I ain't so sure," Jace said stubbornly.

"Well, I am," Rufe declared, and drumming his horse in the ribs with his heels, started down the long, gentle grade for the homestead.

Leo followed at once, catching up quickly, as did the others. When they drew near, they saw several figures working in a garden that lay alongside the farmhouse, and then, as they rode even closer, the figures took on definition and became women.

"I don't see no menfolk around," Fargo remarked.

"Expect they're out in the fields somewhere," Rufe said. "Makes it real easy for us. Can go in, fill our bellies with good grub, rest up by that spring till it cools off, then move on."

"I just might even hang around a mite longer," Leo said, grinning as he eyed the women.

Rufe slanted a look at Jenny Waring. "Yeh, maybe we both'll do just that."

They reached the edge of the yard, a large, neatly cleared hard-pack area behind which stood the main farmhouse and several smaller structures. The women, four of them — two elderly and two fairly young — had ceased hoeing and were watching them narrowly.

"Howdy, ladies," Rufe sang out in his customary disarming way. "This is a mighty pretty place you all've got here. Expect your menfolk are still working."

"They're around," one of the younger women replied. Each of them was wearing a large sunbonnet that all but hid their faces.

"Around," Leo repeated, "around here close — or where?"

"What do you want?" another of the women, one much older than the first, asked in a suspicious voice. "We ain't got no money if you're looking to rob us."

"That ain't what we're wanting," Leo said, gaze still centered on the young one.

"That's right, ma'am," Rufe added. "We're just pilgrims headed for the border, and we don't aim to hurt nobody. Just thought maybe you'd fix us up with a good supper. Been a long time since we had us a —"

"You've got a girl there with you," the elderly woman said. "Can't she cook?"

"Nope, she sure ain't much of a hand at doing that."

The woman gave that a bit of thought, turned, said something to the others. Somewhere over behind the main house the shrill voices of children at play could be heard. Abruptly the younger woman spoke.

"You best keep going — we don't want strangers around here. Can water your horses at the spring, then move on."

Leo spurred his horse, rushed forward, pointing directly for her. "Now, that ain't very sociable! I was figuring that me and you'd —"

A rifle cracked from among the trees near the spring. Leo stiffened, drew himself up in the saddle as his horse came to a stop, and then fell heavily to the ground.

Rufe yelled, dragged out his pistol. "Them damned sodbusters — they've gone and shot Leo!" he yelled, and fired at the women, all now running for the house.

One paused, fell as a bullet struck her.

Instantly more shots erupted from the trees. Jace Fargo winced as a slug tore into his side. Rufe, horse shying wildly, cursed, emptied his weapon at the unseen riflemen in the trees.

"Get out of here!" he yelled suddenly, as if realizing the futility of their position, and cut his horse about.

"Leo — what about Leo?" Billy called after him.

"He's dead! Ain't no sense wasting time on him," Rufe answered.

"Leave him be," Fargo added, hand pressed to his side as he veered in close. "Them folks'll bury him."

Bullets were snapping at their clothing, spurting dust all about the hooves of their horses. The women, now inside the house with the exception of the one shot by Rufe, were adding their efforts to those of the riflemen with shotguns.

Jenny, following Rufe across the hard pack, hesitated, beckoned anxiously to Billy, who had halted and was staring fixedly at the body of his brother, sprawled in the dust.

"Come on!" she yelled. "Don't forget us — Mexico!"

23

"It's the Beecham place," Ben Skerrit said in reply to Gurley's question concerning smoke rising to the west and south of them. "Three brothers and their families. Came out here when the war ended and homesteaded. Made a good thing out of it."

It was late in the afternoon. Skerrit had pushed hard despite the heat, hoping to cut Rufe Houston's lead and put himself and Gurley within striking distance of the outlaws.

Time was running out. They were getting close to the border, and while the warden entertained no thoughts of abandoning the chase should Houston and the others reach the line before he could overtake them, he was making every effort to prevent it. A *norteamericano* lawman endeavoring to track down an outlaw in the sandy hills, dense thickets, and sleepy villages of Mexico found the task a near impossibility as cooperation from either the army, the resident police, and the people in general was practically nonexistent.

"We putting up there for the night?" Dave wondered as they began to veer toward the source of the smoke, hidden at that moment by a brush-covered hill.

Skerrit said, "No — can't take the time. Not far to the border. Got to nail Rufe before he can get there."

They reached the hill's crest, dropped off onto its opposite side, and began a long, gradual descent to the hollow in which the Beecham homestead lay.

"They sure picked a fine place," Gurley commented. "Plenty of hay growing in them fields, and they've got a garden and orchard. For sure've got all the water they need."

"There's a spring," Skerrit said absently. He was studying the farm — the yard, the house, the over-all area. It appeared deserted.

"All it ever takes —"

At Gurley's words, Skerrit brushed at the sweat misting his eyes, turned to him. "All what takes?"

"Was saying that water is all it takes in this country to make it bloom. Your friends down there've got a good spring. Plain that it furnishes them with all they need."

"Can't call them my friends — hardly know them," Skerrit said, attention again on the homestead. "Story goes that they owned a big plantation in Mississippi — or one of the Confederate states. The war came along, and like most Southerners, they lost everything. . . . There's something wrong down there, Dave."

Gurley fell silent, centered his interest on the Beecham place. "Kind of looks that way," he said after a few moments. "Ought to see somebody stirring around at this time of day."

"Houston!" Skerrit exclaimed in a sudden, tight voice. "Could be he's been there — or is still hanging around."

Gurley kneed his horse in alongside Skerrit's bay. Shading his eyes against the lowering sun, he scoured the Beecham property with patient, probing eyes. Finished, he shook his head.

"Can't see nobody — no horses — nothing."

"That's what's wrong," Skerrit said. "It's not natural. We best split up, circle in."

Gurley at once swung away. Skerrit said, "Watch yourself," and turned the bay to the opposite direction.

They closed in slowly, Ben's glance sweeping the place constantly, alert for any movement that would betray someone hiding, someone waiting to get him or

Gurley within shooting range.

Abruptly gunshots broke out, the echoes rolling across the hollow and fading into the low hills as bullets spurted sand a few strides in front of the bay. Ben stopped, threw a hurried look at Gurley. The younger man had not been hit either, but the shots, clearly a warning, had brought him to a halt also.

"Don't come no closer!" a voice, coming from the farmhouse, broke the hot silence. "We've had enough of your kind for one day! Keep riding or we'll cut you down!"

The warning could mean but one thing; Rufe Houston and his bunch had been there.

"Hold your fire, Beecham," Skerrit called, lifting his arm with hand palm open and forward. "We're friends."

There was a long minute of silence broken only by the barking of a dog somewhere on the property and the whistling of a meadowlark over in a nearby field.

"I know you?" the voice said then. "Name yourself."

"Skerrit. I'm the warden of the Territorial Prison. Man with me's Dave Gurley. Made him my deputy. We're tracking an escaped convict. Figured him and the bunch with him passed by here on their way to the border."

Again there was quiet. Finally a door opened in the front wall of the house. A man, rifle in his hands, stepped into view.

"Ain't sure I know you — and my brothers ain't sure, either — but come on in," he said. "Best you do it slow and don't make no bad moves. There's a half a dozen guns pointing at both of you."

Skerrit put the bay into motion, saw Gurley follow suit. Together, hands well away from their sides, they covered the remainder of the slope, reached the hard pack, and halted in front of the house. Immediately the man with the rifle stepped farther into the open. Two more, looking much like him but younger, and carrying rifles also, moved out to stand at his shoulders.

"You're the Beechams," Skerrit said. "Stopped by here once before — been a few years ago. Was wearing a star then."

The older brother considered Skerrit coldly. Back inside the house there was the sound of someone weeping. "You got something to prove what you're saying?" he asked. "Talk comes mighty cheap."

Ben, careful, reached into his shirt pocket and drew forth his commission as a deputy sheriff, made out to him by name and as warden of the penitentiary, and handed it to Beecham. The homesteader unfolded the square of paper, read, and then returned it.

"What it says, all right, but how am I to know it's your'n?"

Skerrit, abruptly impatient, swore. Precious minutes were slipping away. "I don't give a damn whether you believe it or not, Beecham. Makes no difference to me. If you had some trouble, I'm interested in knowing if it was Rufe Houston and his bunch —"

"Had trouble, all right! Wife's dead and one of the girls is shot up. But we —"

"Sorry about your womenfolk," Skerrit cut in. "Houston's a big man. Last we heard he was still wearing prison clothes. Would've been four others with him — one of them a young girl."

"It was them," another of the Beechams said. "Only there ain't but four of them now, all told." He paused, pointed off to a hillside. "We buried one of them over there."

The anger that gripped Ben Skerrit as he listened to the recounting mounted steadily. The outlaws had killed again — this time a woman. But they hadn't gotten off free. One of them had paid the price — in full. "One less to contend with," he thought, and then a surge of anxiety possessed him. Was it Rufe the Beechams had killed? Was he going to be cheated out of his vengeance?

"Which one was he?" he asked, glancing at all three of the Beechams in turn. "Houston was a big man — like I said. He's in his forties and —"

"Weren't him," the eldest Beecham cut in. "This'n weren't much more'n a boy. Was maybe twenty."

Skerrit heaved a silent sigh of relief. Rufe was still alive — and his.

"How long ago were they here?"

"Couple, three hours at most. We was coming in from the south hay field — me and my brothers. Was quitting early. Heard them ride up, talking big. Womenfolk were there in the garden. They told them they wasn't welcome; we been having a peck of trouble with tramps and outlaws going to or coming up from Mexico.

"They didn't pay no mind, and the one that I put a bullet in started getting smart with my brother Joe's wife, Amy. Was me that shot him — and I ain't sorry. It's the only way to handle trash like them. Bad thing about it is they went and opened up on the women."

Skerrit listened in silence. He heard Gurley swear deeply, glanced at him, nodded. They were having the same bitter thought, "Get Houston before he can murder again." Grim, he turned back to the homesteaders.

"They head south when they rode out?"

The oldest of the trio nodded. Two women had now appeared in the doorway, one holding a small child, and were listening to what was being said.

"Was when they left here. Expect they was aiming for the Mexican border, but they could've cut east through the brakes for Texas."

Skerrit had forgotten about that particular section of the country — one of ragged arroyos, brushy hills, and bluffs that extended in a wide band across the lower part of the territory. It was a discouraging recollection. He had thought to ride hard and fast in a direct line for Mexico and eventually overtake the outlaws; now they would have to resort to tracking, making certain they were on their trail and thus be slowed down greatly.

"Them horses of your'n look pretty beat," the senior Beecham said. "Be willing to loan you a couple if you like, seeing as how it's them killers you're after."

Skerrit nodded. "Be a big help — a favor —"

"Can leave yours here, pick them up on the way back," the homesteader continued, and then added realistically, "If'n you don't make it back, I reckon we won't be out nothing. The trade'll be about even up."

Skerrit grinned, stepped down from the bay. "We'll appreciate this. Important we catch that bunch, and we can, with fresh horses."

"Just what I was thinking," Beecham said. "Just follow me around back. Can pick yourself a animal from them there in the barnyard. . . . Maybe if people'd pitch in and kill off them renegades every time they showed up somewhere, this country'd be safe for decent folks."

24

"Rufe, I'm hurting bad. I've got to fix this here hole in my side."

Jace Fargo's voice was a piteous wail. They had been riding steadily for over an hour, their tired horses doing the best they could in the closing darkness.

"Can't stop," Houston shouted back. "Could be we're being chased. I want to reach that brush on a ways so's we can duck out of sight. Won't take more'n a few minutes."

Fargo groaned, clutched his wounded side tightly. The large-caliber bullet had entered his body just below the rib cage, and the wound was bleeding profusely.

"I — I can't hold out — much longer —"

Rufe looked over his shoulder, searched the trail behind them. He could see no one — no signs of pursuit — but he was not convinced. Those damn homesteaders were tricky — hadn't they proved it by lying in ambush back there and then opening fire when nobody was looking for it? Like as not they were coming on fast, only they were keeping out of sight so's they'd not be seen.

Rufe cursed angrily, swung his attention to Jace, then to the girl and finally Billy. Why the hell hadn't it been Billy the hayseed bastards had killed instead of Leo? Billy, if he lived to be a hundred, would never amount to half the man Leo was. Damn it all, anyway!

Just what was going on? Why had everything all of a sudden gone wrong? Things were moving along fine, just fine: the break at the pen, the clean escape even after Billy messed things up so's they'd not have horses to leave on. Even that hadn't been too much of a setback. They'd been able to get horses and everything else they needed at that store.

After that they'd run into that pilgrim headed for Arizona and later on those two cowhands — and everything had worked out smooth as corn silk. Luck had been with them when they stopped at that town, Haystack, too. The two lawmen who had somehow gotten on their trail were spotted by Leo — by God, it was going to be hell not having that boy around to depend on — and he was able to slip away with the others before the tin stars could make their move.

"Rufe —"

Rufe slowed his lagging horse, veered in to Fargo. "It ain't far," he said. "Them bluffs — just up ahead."

Fargo moaned. "I can't hang on much longer. Head's kind of light and I ain't seeing so good. This here horse, too, is about to cave in."

"They all are, Pa," Billy said, drawing in close. "We've got to pull up."

"We'll do what I say — and when I say!" Rufe shouted, instantly angry.

"If these horses give out under us, you won't have no say-so," Billy retorted.

Rufe's face flushed and his eyes hardened. He waited a long breath and then said, "They'll hold out for another mile or so. . . . And you watch your lip, boy, or I'll make you wish you was never borned!"

Billy glanced at Jenny. In the weak light of ending day her face was a pale oval beneath the old hat she was wearing. She smiled encouragingly.

"Nope — not ever again, Pa," he said, looking directly at Rufe. "You ain't never again laying a hand on me."

Rufe spat, considered his son coldly. "Oh, I expect I will — maybe soon as we get to them bluffs and fix up Jace. . . . Sure a shame it was Leo that got shot. A pity it wasn't you."

Billy stiffened, and then he looked down. "Yeh, that what you would've liked, Pa. Was always Leo you favored."

"Because he was a man, that's why. Always done what I told him — and done it right."

"That's what you thought, but Leo was real smart. He made it look that way to you, but what he was doing was playing you for a sucker."

"Don't you go bad-mouthing him! I won't let you — I'll shoot you right off'n that saddle!"

"I reckon you would, Pa, if it would help Leo any, but I'm through giving a damn about it. I'm pulling out — me and Jenny. We're taking off on our own."

"The hell you are!" Rufe shouted. "You're staying right with me till I say you can go!"

"No, Pa — and you can't stop us —"

"I sure'n hell can! You try riding off and I'll put a bullet in the girl before you can get ten feet! Not in you — but in her. Seems she's come to mean something to you, so you'd best listen to me unless you want her dead."

"He's just talking, Billy," Jenny called from her place beside the suffering Fargo. "Anyway, I'm willing to take the chance."

Billy, pale eyes studying Rufe, was silent for a long minute, and then he shook his head.

"I ain't," he said. "I know him — he'd do it. Killing don't mean nothing to him. Best we play it safe. . . . How long do we have to stay around, Pa?"

"Till I get them damned hayshakers off'n my tail —"

Billy frowned, swiped at the sweat shining on his face. "You ain't even sure they're chasing us!"

"They are — can bet on it. A couple of their women got shot, so they'll be coming to even the score. Ain't you wanting to go on to Mexico, get some of that gold?"

"Sure, but the way things are happening it's beginning to look like it ain't going to work out. All there is to it is talk — and me and Jenny ain't interested in talk — and now if Jace dies —"

"He ain't going to die."

"Maybe not. You going to stop somewhere, wait for them sodbusters? That what you're figuring to do?"

Rufe nodded, pointed. "Them bluffs right on ahead. Aim to find a good place along the trail, set up a ambush. Then, when they come along, I'm — we're going to blow their damn heads off. It'll have to be me and you. Jace ain't in no shape to shoot — and Leo's gone."

"After that me and Jenny can go on — that it?"

Rufe shrugged. "You can both go straight to hell for all I give a hoot," he said.

Billy laughed. "I'm obliged to you, Pa. For once I'm glad it was Leo you favored and not me."

The bluffs were before them. Rufe, ignoring Billy's comment, urged his weary horse forward and began to search the darkness for a place to lay his ambush. Shortly he cut off the trail into a pocket created by a ragged-faced cliff on one side, tall mesquite and briar bush on the other.

"This here'll do fine," he said, his voice lifting almost joyfully. "I can set up there on the point of the bluff and see them coming."

Fargo muttered unintelligibly as he pulled in beside Rufe. He started to dismount, lost his stirrup, and fell to the ground with a groan.

"Damn it!" Rufe shouted, and dismounting, hurried to the man's side. "Billy, you take them horses off into that brush and tie them up — and you sure better tie them good this time! Girl, you come here, help me with Jace. And bring one of them canteens of water."

They did the best they could for Fargo, cleaning his wound with water, disinfecting it by pouring a bit of whiskey onto the raw flesh, and then binding it with a bandage made from Jenny's petticoat. But the outlaw had lost far too much blood, and even a good swallow of the whiskey failed to restore any degree of strength.

"Maybe come daylight he'll perk up," Rufe said. "Could be resting and sleeping'll do him good. Just let him lay there quiet."

Rufe paused, rubbed at his jaw. The night was now complete, and light from the moon and stars flooded the land. He nodded to Jenny Waring.

"I'm going up on top of the bluff so's I can keep a eye out for them sodbusters. I want you to come along and keep me company."

"No, Pa, she ain't doing it," Billy said flatly before the girl could give an answer. "Jenny's mine and you ain't going to touch her. Me and you'll fight first."

Rufe considered that for a few moments, shrugged. "So be it. Far as I'm concerned, she ain't worth fighting for — especially at a time like this," he said, and moving on, worked his way up the fairly steep slope until he had gained the top. "Can sure see fine from here."

"That's good, Pa," Billy said in a disinterested voice, and taking Jenny by the hand, sat down near Jace Fargo.

"Reckon we better be making some plans," Rufe heard Billy say. "And waiting like this'll be a mighty good time to do it. I ain't forgot what you said about us teaming up."

"Didn't figure you had after hearing what you said to your pa. Anyway, I didn't aim to let you," Jenny replied. After a bit she added, "I'm so sleepy. Seems we ain't been doing nothing but travel, day and night."

"Don't you go building no fire down there!" Rufe warned from above. "I don't want them jaspers spotting us."

"All right, Pa, there won't be no fire," Billy said, and then as if it had suddenly come to mind, continued, "Pa, I want to ask you a question."

"Yeh?" Rufe's voice was deep, strong, showed no signs of the fatigue that gripped the others.

"Like for you to tell me why you was always favoring Leo over me. Wondered about it a many a time. I could work just as good as him, shoot and ride, too, only he was always taking the credit. Why, Pa, why was it?"

In the hush that followed Billy's words, the distant barking of coyotes was clear, sharp. Rufe hawked, spat. "Well, boy, I'll tell you for true, since you're asking. I never was sure you was mine — my own son."

Billy raised his head slowly, looked up to the top of the bluff. Rufe was a dark, partly visible silhouette against the sky.

"You saying you ain't my pa?"

"Said I was never for certain. I was gone for a spell, and when I come back, you'd been borned. Didn't figure out exactly right, but your ma said I was wrong, that I was your pa. Didn't make no difference, so I let it ride."

Billy shook his head. "Did make a difference, and you know it."

"Well, maybe, but there ain't nothing I can do about it now. Want you to hush up, quit your yammering. A man's voice can carry plenty far on a night like this."

"I'm sort of glad you told me — about me," Billy said, ignoring the caution. "Glad I ain't yours, that you ain't my pa. And I'm glad too that I know why you treated me the way you did. Proves I wasn't your blood. . . . Did Leo know?"

"Nope, never told him. . . . Now, shut up and get some sleep. We've done enough talking."

"Yeh, I reckon we have."

Rufe Houston settled back, shoulders against a hump on the crest of the bluff. He intended to stay awake, but after a while he dozed, fitfully at the start, and then, near morning, fell into a sound slumber. He came awake abruptly at first light. What aroused him he had no idea, but he immediately saw two riders coming up the trail leading into the brakes.

"Figured there'd be more'n two of them damned sodbusters after me," he muttered. "Hell, had I knowed I'd a' waited and took care of them a long time ago."

Then it came to him; they were not from the homestead — they were the two lawmen he thought he'd eluded back at Haystack! Moments later, when the riders drew nearer, he altered that conclusion.

"Them ain't lawmen! That's the warden, and the kid of that screw, Gurley! They're the ones that've been dogging me. Well, I got a mighty nice little surprise fixed up for them."

Grinning broadly, Rufe stretched out full length on the crest of the bluff, and, pistol ready, waited.

25

"Right up there, on top of that bluff," Skerrit said. "Can't point — and don't let on like we've spotted him. He could be watching us."

It was just daylight. Skerrit and Gurley had ridden as far as they dared that previous night, and then halted. It was not because of their horses; the ones they were now riding, borrowed from the Beechams, were fresh; it was simply that they had lost the outlaws' trail, and despite the strong moonlight, neither Gurley nor the warden had been able to pick it up.

"Soon as we reach the tall brush ahead," Skerrit said, "you cut off and circle around behind him. I've got a hunch they've made camp nearby — probably at the foot of the bluff."

"You waiting here?"

"No, I'll keep going till I reach that brush on the right. I'll hole up there, watch for you. When I see you on the other side, I'll signal, and we can move in on them together. . . . Want to remind you again,

Dave — Rufe belongs to me."

Gurley nodded. "And I'm reminding you — if you miss, I won't," he said.

They had reached the tangle of mesquite, were below Rufe Houston's line of vision. Gurley veered from the trail, began to circle the ragged formation, which detached from a larger embankment, was more in the nature of a butte.

Skerrit, nerves taut, a coolness flowing through him, proceeded along the path at a slow, quiet walk, taking a moment during the time he was beyond the outlaw's sight to draw his pistol, check the loads, and make certain it was ready. Finally he had caught up with Rufe Houston, and retribution was at hand. Dave Gurley was hoping that his aim would not be true. It would never happen. The outlaw was going to die — and by his gun.

The trail, now cutting its way through dense brush, had narrowed. Skerrit, keeping well to the left side, where he knew Houston's view of his approach would be limited and completely blocked at times, was endeavoring to gauge Dave Gurley's movements and figure when he would reach the far side of the bluff. He was unfamiliar with the area, could only guess as to its actual lay. But he reckoned

Gurley's course would be a short one since the butte itself was not large.

Abruptly the trail broke out into the open. Skerrit, hanging tight to his nerves and suppressing an impulse to look toward the point where Rufe was hiding, kept his eyes straight ahead. He was getting dangerously near to the outlaw, wished again that he could see some indication of Gurley's position.

Two quail suddenly rocketed out from the brush to his right. Skerrit jumped, pulled back. He grinned tightly, continued, still keeping to the thick growth as much as possible. Again the trail dipped and he was once more out of the outlaw's sight, but he was now almost opposite the butte. When the trail opened up again, he would be abreast the formation and Rufe Houston would have a clear shot at him.

It would work both ways: he would have an open line at the outlaw, and picking him off the top of the butte would be easy, like knocking a bottle off a fence post. Tension increased within Ben Skerrit. A few more steps and that moment would be at hand.

Far off in the brake to the west a mockingbird was offering a melodic imitation to the rising sun. Skerrit, moving slow, cautiously, listened absently for several moments, but his eyes were on the break in the brush ahead where he knew he would come out into the open. He had no fixed plan as to what he would do; at such times, and in unfamiliar country, a man could do little more than react, trusting in his instincts to bring him safely through.

Relief coursed through Skerrit. Gurley had appeared in the brush near the base of the butte. Dave caught sight of him at almost the identical time, had lifted his hand to indicate he was ready. Skerrit nodded, continued his slow approach.

He reached the break in the trail, halted. He looked again to Gurley, partly hidden now by a bulge in the butte. Taut, Skerrit gathered his muscles, tensed, and lunged suddenly into the open.

"Rufe!" he yelled. "Throw down your gun!"

"Throw it down!" Gurley echoed from his position opposite.

Rufe Houston, on his knees, with arm raised and pistol trained on Skerrit, hesitated. He glanced from Skerrit to Gurley, and then again to the warden, completely surprised to find one of them in front of him, the other at his back. Slowly, he lowered his weapon.

"You got me!" he called hoarsely. "I give up."

Skerrit eyed the outlaw narrowly. It was too easy. Rufe knew what lay ahead for him, and it wasn't likely he'd quit that quickly.

"Don't shoot!" Rufe yelled. "I'm coming down."

Before Skerrit could order the outlaw to wait, Rufe slid from the top of the butte. Alarmed, the warden lunged through the brush for the hollow he figured was at its base, and where the rest of the party — the older man, the boy, and the Waring girl, hopefully being covered by Dave Gurley — would be. He reached it, pulled up short.

Crouched in the center of the small clearing was Rufe Houston. He had his pistol in his hand, was holding the muzzle of the barrel to the head of the Waring girl. Nearby lay a man of about the outlaw's own age, dead, judging from the color and slackness of his features. Evidently he had taken one of the Beecham family's bullets.

The third member — young, lean, with light eyes and hair — was standing just beyond the grinning Rufe; arms partly raised before the threat of Gurley's pistol, he was frowning as he stared at Rufe.

"Looks like we got us a Mexican standoff, Warden," Rufe said. "You or that kid of old Gurley's makes a move, and I'll put a bullet in the gal's head!"

"And I'll put one in this boy of yours," Dave Gurley warned. "He is your son, ain't he?"

"Maybe," Rufe said. "Don't matter nohow. I'm backing out of here and getting my horse — over there in the brush — and I'm taking this here little gal along so's you won't try following me. If I see you on my trail, she's dead. Savvy?"

"No, you ain't taking her no place!" the boy yelled, and ignoring Gurley, threw himself at Rufe.

Rufe pivoted. Hanging on to the girl, he shifted his pistol, fired. The bullet struck the boy in the chest, slammed him back against the face of the butte.

In almost that same instant Rufe triggered his weapon again — this time at Skerrit. He fired too fast. His aim was only fair. The warden flinched as the bullet grooved his arm. The outlaw's gun came up for another try. Gurley triggered his pistol in that fragment of time. Houston yelled as a leg gave out from under him. He grabbed for the disabled member, releasing his grip on the girl and dropping his weapon as he went down.

Skerrit, pistol cocked and leveled at the outlaw, moved in slowly. His sights were centered on Rufe's head, his finger rested lightly on the trigger. Nearby Dave Gurley was waiting, gun also ready. The girl, standing in the midst of the drifting clouds of powder smoke, suddenly free of being in the center of the shooting, began to scream as shock overcame her, sending echoes racing out across the brushy hills and up the arroyos.

"Shoot, damn you! Shoot!"

Rufe Houston's voice cut through the girl's shrill screaming. Skerrit nodded, his mouth pulled into a tight line. He started to speak, to answer the outlaw; tell him it was the reason he and Gurley had trailed him and his bunch for days — so that he would have the pleasure of killing him, removing him so that he could never again take another's life.

But the words wouldn't come; they simply weren't there. He was realizing, instead, that to do so he would debase himself, that it would lower him to the same level as Rufe Houston, and he couldn't live with that thought.

"No, I'm not about to," he said, glancing at Gurley and shaking his head warningly. "It'd be too good for you. I'm going to hang you, personally, when we get back to the pen. I want every man there to have the satisfaction of watching you gag and choke when we put the rope around your neck, and hear the snap when your neck breaks —"

"No!" Rufe yelled. "No, not hanging! Shoot me now, Warden, here and now. I ain't never begged no man for nothing, but I'm begging you —"

"Forget it, Rufe. You're going to swing, and John Gurley's boy there's going to be standing right beside me when I pull the trap —"

"No!" the outlaw shouted again, and lunged for his pistol, laying a yard beyond his reach.

Jenny Waring, the moments of shock passed and now in control of herself, was standing just beyond him. She moved forward quickly, kicked the weapon off into the brush, well clear of his groping fingers. Rufe cursed, lay back, gripped his bleeding leg.

Skerrit turned his attention to Dave Gurley. "You with me in this, or am I going to have trouble with you?"

A hard smile cracked Gurley's lips. "Long as you'll do what you said you would with him, I reckon I'm with you."

The warden smiled. "Never gone back on my word yet, don't aim to start now —

especially over him. Let's get squared around here and head back. You bring up the horses, I'll see to trussing up Rufe."

"What about the dead ones — and the girl?"

"We'll pack them back to the Beechams, ask them to do the burying. Girl can stay with them or ride on to Capital City with us," Skerrit said, and glanced at the girl. "You got any relatives around?"

Jenny shook her head. "I'll stay with those folks for a while, if they'll let me, then I'll go on to somewheres else." She paused, looked down at Billy. "We was going to team up, but that's all over now."

Skerrit nodded, turned away as Gurley started to go for the horses. Rufe Houston stirred, swore raggedly.

"Ain't you going to fix my leg some? It's busted, and it's still bleeding."

"Aim to put a bandage on it soon as I can fix one. Need one for myself —"

"And riding a horse, that'll kill me, setting a saddle all the way back to the pen!"

Ben Skerrit smiled. "Nope, it won't kill you, Rufe. I won't let it. I'm saving you for a hanging."

We hope you have enjoyed this Large Print book. Other Thorndike, Wheeler or Chivers Press Large Print books are available at your library or directly from the publishers.

For more information about current and upcoming titles, please call or write, without obligation, to:

Publisher
Thorndike Press
295 Kennedy Memorial Drive
Waterville, ME 04901
Tel. (800) 223-1244

Or visit our Web site at:
www.gale.com/thorndike
www.gale.com/wheeler

OR

Chivers Large Print
published by BBC Audiobooks Ltd
St James House, The Square
Lower Bristol Road
Bath BA2 3BH
England
Tel. +44(0) 800 136919
email: bbcaudiobooks@bbc.co.uk
www.bbcaudiobooks.co.uk

All our Large Print titles are designed for easy reading, and all our books are made to last.